WELCOME TO THE
JEFF DAVIS CAMEL CORPS

The new motion, coupled with the hot sun, made it impossible for Caldwell to do more than swallow the green taste in his mouth and hang on for dear life. The only ray of hope he saw in this ghastly ride from the river was that at this rate it would soon be over. The fort was much nearer now, and he had to admit a camel crossed a lot of country in a hurry. The animal he rode stood at least six feet at the shoulder. Higher yet, up here on the hump. Those long legs gave it nearly twice the stride of any horse, and if what they said about them going nine days between waterings was true, he could see certain advantages to Secretary Davis's wild-sounding scheme.

If only, he added with a groan, somebody could teach the goddamn things to move in a straight line like reasonable animals!

THE SPIRIT HORSES

LOU CAMERON

Ⓒ

CHARTER BOOKS, NEW YORK

THE SPIRIT HORSES

A Charter Book / published by arrangement with
the author

PRINTING HISTORY
Ballantine edition / June 1976
Charter edition / November 1986

ISBN: 0-441-77809-7

Charter Books are published by The Berkley Publishing Group,
200 Madison Avenue, New York, New York 10016.
PRINTED IN THE UNITED STATES OF AMERICA

AUGUST 19, 1857 . . . The steamboat *Mojave Belle* clawed chocolate-colored mud from the shallow bottom as she threaded her way between the sandbars of the Lower Colorado. On the forward Texas deck, Second Lieutenant Matthew Caldwell stared morosely upstream, an unlit cigar gripped between his teeth as he tried to ignore the sweaty discomfort of his dress blues. He'd spent most of the river voyage up from Fort Yuma naked in the relative comfort of his cabin, but some idiot had yelled, over an hour ago, that they were arriving at Havasu, and he, like another idiot, had gotten dressed to report properly to his new post.

There was nothing like an army post in sight, and the afternoon sun, adding the humidity of the river to the desert's dry heat, was unbearable. The Colorado ran between steep adobe banks, but from the Texas deck Matt Caldwell could see the dead, flat desolation on either side. There were faint gray-purple mountains in the shimmering distance, but for mile after monotonous mile the Colorado Desert seemed a dull, uninteresting corner of hell. When they told him, back at Fort Leavenworth, that he'd been posted to the "Great American Desert," Caldwell had expected something like those pictures he'd seen in Captain Burton's books about the Sahara. A desert was a place where golden moons shone down on shifting white dunes, or a cool oasis surrounded by exotic palm trees. But this country had no sand dunes. No date palms. Just an endless expanse of knee-high scrub, growing from a flat, gray pavement of birdcage gravel. His orders read that he was posted to Campbell's Dragoons and his new duties

1

would involve guarding the ford near the head of navigation and patrolling the surrounding desert against hostile Indians. It seemed obvious there had to be a fording somewhere up ahead. The river was already shallow enough to ride across in places. But what was that nonsense about hostile Indians? No Indian, or anyone else, could possibly live in country like this.

A voice at Matt's side said, "You need a light fer that *see*-gar, sonny?" and the officer turned his head to take in the long, lean form of a civilian in white cotton clothes and a straw sombrero. He'd noticed the civilian and his naked Indian companion boarding the steamboat at Fort Yuma. The Indian didn't seem to be anywhere in sight, so Caldwell smiled wolfishly and said, "My name is Caldwell, Matt Caldwell. Call me sonny again, and I'll have to lick you fair and square."

The civilian smiled back, which took the edge off the brag as he opined, "I don't lick easy, uh, Matt, but no offense intended. I'm calt Digger. Digger Greenberg. I'm scoutin' fer your old army these days, so me and Rabbit-Boss must be headed fer the same place as your ownself."

"You're joining Campbell's Dragoons at Fort Havasu?"

"Yep, Lord willin' and the river don't git no lower. We'da been there by now, had Yaponcha seed fit to put a mite more water under this old tub's keel, but what the hell, if we run aground, it ain't too fur to walk." The scout peered upstream through the shimmering sunlight on the water and added, "Cain't be more'n six or eight miles from the camp, but you purely talk funny. What was that thing you calt the outfit jest now?"

"Campbell's Dragoons. That's the unit posted at Fort Havasu, isn't it?"

Digger Greenberg shook his head, laughing, and gasped, "Is that what your orders read? Do Jesus! I been wonderin' how in blue blazes they git folks to volunteer fer sech a loco outfit, and now I know. They git you there by spellin' it wrong!"

"It's not Campbell's Dragoons?"

"Shoot, no, sonny, I mean, Matt, it's the Third Dragoons, U.S. *Camel Corps!* Ain't you never heard of the U.S. Camel Corps?"

Matt Caldwell's face was carefully blank as he said, "I think I might have read something about the experiment in the *Army Times* back in Leavenworth. I, uh, didn't know they'd actually *done* anything about Secretary Davis's, uh . . ."

"Crazy notion!" Greenberg filled in. "I can say Jefferson Davis is crazy if I've a mind to, on account I ain't swore in as a sojer and I ain't about to be, as long as Buchanan picks hombres like that'n to be his Secretary of War!"

Matt Caldwell said, "Let's not get into politics just now. Are you serious about them actually having *camels* at Fort Havasu?"

"Well, I can't hardly take one of them critters serious, but they sure as hell have a mess of 'em where we're headed. Got, oh, I'd say two dozen of the varmints at Havasu. Got some others over to the Californee gold fields to the west. You let a muley hombre like Jeff Davis take a notion betwixt his teeth and there's no tellin' what in hell he might do!"

Matt Caldwell didn't answer as he considered the scout's words. It was entirely possible the man was greening him, Matt knew. As a shavetail from the East, albeit overage in grade, he was a likely target for the not-too-subtle joshing of the self-styled forty-niners.

On the other hand, President Buchanan's flamboyant Secretary of War was known for his lively imagination and sometimes bizarre orders. The fiery Democrat from Mississippi had turned the Regular Army upside down since taking over as Secretary of War, and in truth, some of his ideas for the settlement of the territories recently taken from Mexico hadn't been as impractical as his enemies in Congress had made them out to be.

Caldwell, as a Free-stater, was opposed to the Southern Democrat in charge of the War Department on political as well as personal grounds. If he'd been transferred to this remote outpost for the reason he was beginning to suspect, Jefferson Davis and his Mississippi clique in Washington were guilty of more than partisan politics. But to give the devil his due, some of the changes Davis had made in the frontier army were reasonable. His pacification of the Comanche and Apache raiders had been firm but fair, and the overland route between Texas and the California gold fields seemed secure. His suggestion for a pony express along the Gila–Rio Grande route by way of Apache Pass had been blocked by his Northern opposition in Congress, but that didn't mean the idea was impractical; it only meant the Abolitionists suspected the "empire builder's" motives in pushing for a southern route for the overland mail, telegraph, and possible railroad links across the vast new territories.

Matt Caldwell had good reason of his own to suspect the Secretary of ulterior motives, but again to give the devil his due, Jeff Davis was neither mad nor inept, and the French *were* using camels in *their* new desert empire. Still . . .

"My orders distinctly read Campbell's Dragoons," he told Digger Greenberg. "I suppose it could have been taken down the wrong way when it came over the telegraph wire from Washington, but . . ."

Greenberg cut in. "Don't matter how them telegraph Johnnies writ it down. The critters up to Havasu is camels. I seed them my ownself last time me and Rabbit-Boss was up this way scoutin' fer Captain Lodge." He spit over the rail and conceded, "I'll allow as how it's hard to believe. The remount service has a joke about a camel bein' a horse as was made up by a committee. But that's what they've assigned as mounts at Fort Havasu. Jeff Davis was so keen on

4

the way Louis Napoleon's Frenchified Furren Legion has been tear-assin' all over Al-jerry with the critters that he up and bought hisself a passel offen the Turks in a town calt Smyrna. Hombre calt Porter, Lieutenant Porter, brung 'em all the way in a boat with holes cut in the deck fer their long, scrawny ol' necks an' wound up ahead of the game when a couple was born on the boat comin' over."

Caldwell nodded. It hardly seemed possible this semiliterate mountain man could have made up the part about Louis Napoleon, though it was known that Secretary Davis was an unabashed admirer of Louis Napoleon's Second Empire. The new U.S. Infantry caps being issued at the moment were directly copied from the kepis of the French Foreign Legion.

Still, one never knew, west of the Big Muddy. These unwashed and bearded types out here were given to tall tales of skunk eggs, lost white tribes, lakes of washing soda, and trees two hundred feet high. He'd wait to see about the mounts at Fort Havasu. Meanwhile, where in blazes *was* his new post?

As if in answer to his unspoken question, the *Mojave Belle*'s tinny steam whistle bleated helplessly, and Caldwell realized they'd stopped moving upstream. The little steamboat's stern paddle churned in futile desperation as the blunt bow simply refused to scrape the bottom any farther. Up in the bow, a Mexican crewman, naked to the waist, ran forward with a lead line to sound the channel. He tossed the lead, turned his head, and yelled up to the pilot, *"Aqui no agua! Es finito!"* Then, since the afternoon sun was very hot, and since nobody was going anyplace anyway, the Mexican jumped overboard into the knee-deep water and began to splash happily in the shallows.

The pilot came out on the Texas deck to order the crewman back aboard, but by this time the Mexican had been joined by three others and a couple of Indian passengers from the steerage deck. The pilot

5

swore to himself and walked aft to find some shade and a cool drink. Matt Caldwell turned to the civilian scout at his side and asked, "What do we do now?"

Greenberg shrugged. "We wait fer them to miss us and send a patrol downstream, we wait till dark and walk it in the coolth, or we pray to Yaponcha fer high water."

"That's the second time you've mentioned this, ah ... Ya-whosits?"

"Yaponcha, the Storm Spirit. This is the Storm Moon, you know. The Diggers say Yaponcha wakes in late summer and roams the high country, bangin' thunderheads agin' the mountaintops and greenin' the piñon trees fer his little brothers, the Injuns. You let old Yaponcha sprinkle the canyon lands to the north a mite, and we'll have us enough water hereabouts to steam the *U.S.S. Pennsylvania* up to Havasu!"

Down on the steerage deck, Greenberg's companion, Rabbit-Boss, was now in sight, standing near the bow with his arms outstretched and his face to the northern sky. Greenberg said, "Old Rabbit-Boss has the same idea. He don't cotton all that much to walkin' at night through Mojave country, neither."

"I thought the Mojave were peaceful Indians."

"They is, to *ussen*. They gener'ly kill ever' Digger they kin git their hands on. Old Rabbit-Boss don't think all that much of them neither. I reckon, next to an Apache, there's nobody a Digger hates worse'n a Mojave."

Caldwell studied the Indian on the lower deck before he answered. Rabbit-Boss was a lean, very dark man who wore nothing but an odd headdress of antelope horns, and a flat basket slung on one hip via a leather thong over one shoulder. He held a carved stick in one hand, and as the young officer watched, Rabbit-Boss waved the stick in time to his soft, singsong incantation, if incantation it was.

Caldwell asked, "What's that he's singing?" and the scout replied, "Rain chant. Ain't no sensible words to

6

it. It'd come out, 'Hey, Storm Spirit, hey Storm Spirit hey, Storm Spirit . . . iffen it was sung in our lingo."

"Do you speak his dialect?"

"Some. He talks English better'n I talk Digger, but I kin make myself understood to most of the desert tribes."

"Most? Not all?"

"Shoot, ain't *nobody* talks to ever' tribe. Most of the Diggers talk Shoshoni, Paiute, Walapai, Snake, and sech. It's all purdy much the same lingo, and Rabbit-Boss says names like Ute and Paiute and Walapai is jest a crazy notion of us white folks. He says nobody lives in the desert except his folks, who talk like him, and the Saltu, who don't."

"I've never heard of a Saltu tribe."

"That's on account there ain't no Saltu tribe. A Saltu is a stranger and outsider—what my grandaddy back in the old country calt a *goy.*"

Caldwell had been wondering about the background of the garrulous scout. Greenberg was a rawboned type with dark, nondescript features half hidden by the unkempt hair on his head and face. Caldwell asked, "What old country would that be, Mister Greenberg?" and the scout said, "A country calt Frankfurt. I was borned on the Red River of the North. My ma was Cree and French-Canuck. My daddy was an Astorian. Afore he was an Astorian, he'd been a Jew from the same old country as John Jacob Astor and all the other Astorians come from. Anyway, my daddy minded some of the old country ways and he tolt me once how his folks calt everbody that warn't a Jew a *goy,* jest like Diggers call ever'body who ain't one of their own a Saltu. I had a Mormon tell me one time that the Injuns was a lost tribe of Jews. So I reckon I got Jew on my ma's side, too."

Caldwell managed to keep a straight face. "Do you, uh, practice the Hebrew faith, Mister Greenberg?"

The scout spit over the rail again. "I boil my drinkin' water, keep a good edge on my barlow knife, and sleep with a small fire and loaded gun. West of Apache Pass, good sense beats prayin' any day of the week!"

As if his companion's words had reached him, the chanting Indian on the lower deck turned, looked up at Greenberg, and called, "The Spirit Horses come. Many of them. As many as the fingers on both hands."

Greenberg nodded and told Caldwell, "They must have spotted the smoke from our stack up to the fort. We're way overdue and they know it's low water."

Caldwell strained his eyes at the wavering horizon area—there was no true horizon at this time of the year on the Colorado Desert—and asked Greenberg, "Can you see a patrol out there? I'll be damned if I can see a thing!"

"I'd be wastin' my time feedin' Rabbit-Boss iffen you could!" The scout smiled. "That old boy's a caution when it comes to sensin' things hereabouts. He hides good, too. I mind one time when me and him was jumped by Mimbres over to the southeast, and he hid me, him, and a damned old mule in a clump of gamma grass you wouldn't have thought a quail coulda hid a nest in."

"Damn it, Greenberg, there's nothing moving out there! The air's sort of, well, shimmering. But there's not a breath of breeze and . . ."

"Look, I don't see nothin' neither, Lieutenant. But take my word fer it, if Rabbit-Boss sees ten camels comin', I'll bet my last bean it won't be nine or eleven! Diggers don't josh much. If he says he sees a camel patrol, a railroad engine, or a elephant a-standin' on its head, it's got to be out there. He's a Rabbit-Boss, not a Dream Singer. No Rabbit-Boss is allowed to see things as ain't there."

The army man strained his eyes, but after a while gave it up as a bad job. He'd had no idea, until he tested his powers of observation, just how hard it was to make a distant object out in the apparently unlimited vista of the open desert. Some of the odd stories of lost immigrant trains were beginning to make sense, if, in fact, there was really a mounted patrol right out there in front of his unseeing eyes.

Greenberg was saying, "Rabbit-Bosses is allowed to see Spirit Lakes, of course. Ever'body sees Spirit Lakes out there on the playas when the sun-ball's high. I seed a *city* out there one time. It was a regular city with church steeples and chimney tops and ever'thing sort of floatin' in the sky above a big old silver lake. I asked Rabbit-Boss did he see it and he said he did, only he didn't want to talk on it. Said it was wrong fer anybody but a Dream Singer to talk on sech things."

"I think you must have seen a mirage. I've read about travelers in North Africa imagining they see water in the desert and . . ."

"Hold on with that imaginin', dang it! I tolt you Rabbit-Boss and me seed the same city and the same lake, didn't I?"

"Well, yes, there's a theory about the desert light being refracted by the heat or something. I'm not sure I understand just how it works."

Greenberg said, "Don't matter how it works. You jest got to know what you're seein' ain't real. Back in forty-nine, a mess of folks got kilt followin' Spirit Lakes offen the trail they shoulda kept to. We still find wagons and sometimes folks out there amidst the playas. Found an hombre last summer, been dead nigh seven years from the papers he had on him. He was still standin', leanin' agin' a joshua tree and starin' out across the playa flats at the Spirit Lake he likely followed fifty miles or more afore he jest dried out and died. Folks as dry out on the playas don't rot, you know. They just shrivel up and turn to leather. I reckon I *do* see the patrol now. Old Rabbit-Boss was right. Eight troopers on ten camels. Reckon they mean the two spares fer you and me."

Caldwell gripped the rail and narrowed his eyes against the glare as he stared hard at the northern emptiness. Was this some obscure western joke? Had this unwashed scout and his naked Indian companion joined in a stupid schoolboy conspiracy to make a fool of him?

And then there was a flash of red and white closer in than he'd been looking, and Caldwell realized with a start that he was looking at a fluttering army guidon. The mounted dragoon who carried the flagstaff was obvious, once you knew where to look and ... good God! There was a column of mounted men in sun-faded blue on tall, ungainly tan animals. Staring, Caldwell said, "That Indian has good eyes. You say his name is Rabbit-Boss?"

"It's more like a title than a name. But I call him that and he knows I mean him. His Digger name is somethin' like Wheat-Shit, which don't sound polite around white folks."

"I see. I don't think I asked what you and Rabbit-Boss are on your way to Fort Havasu for, Mister Greenberg. I mean, are you stationed there or what?"

The scout looked surprised. "Didn't they tell you back at Yuma? Me and Rabbit-Boss has been sent back up here to Havasu fer the same campaign as *you'll* be ridin' out on."

"Campaign? What campaign?"

Greenberg spit again and said, "Well, I reckon they aimed to break it to you gentle."

"Break what to me gentle, damn it? Do you know something I don't know, Greenberg?"

The scout laughed. "I reckon I know a lot you don't, Lieutenant, startin' with knowin' better than to wear a choke collar on the Colorado. But gettin' back to the next day or so, the officer you've been sent to fill in fer wasn't sent home. He kilt his fool self. As to the campaign, I reckon that would be agin' old Diablito and his band. He's been raisin' holy Ned on both sides of the Colorado of late, and I reckon they want us to find the rascal and civilize him with a bullet or two."

The camel patrol was closer now. Caldwell could see that the troopers rode grotesque cruciform saddles, and the lurching gait of the tall beasts was sickening to watch. The camels moved in a long-legged walk rather than a trot or gallop, but they covered ground at a respectable pace. Maybe after he'd had time to familiarize himself with just how you steered one of the damned things . . .

The Mexican crewmen of the steamboat had lined the rail to gape in wonder and prattle in rapid-fire Spanish about the incredible sight of camels in the Colorado Desert. Caldwell had the slight advantage on them in that he knew, at least, what a camel was. Some of the Mexicans were crossing themselves and muttering uneasy prayers as the odd beasts drew nearer and loomed larger. Caldwell had forgotten how *tall* a camel was. The dragoons mounted atop the swaying humps would have a distinct advantage over a mounted horseman in a hand-to-hand skirmish. He said as much to Greenberg, but the scout snorted and said, "Shoot, you caint hardly git one of them critters within a country mile of no self-respectin' horse!"

There was a slight shift in the desert breeze and, as Caldwell gagged on the awful ammonia fumes that suddenly enveloped his head, the scout added, "See what I mean?"

The Mexicans along the rail began to gag and move away, holding noses, cursing, and gasping for air. Greenberg said, "Smells like somebody stuffed one old sweaty sock with limburger cheese and another one with cow shit, don't it?"

Caldwell blinked the tears from his eyes and muttered, "Kee-rist! What are they using for a stable at Havasu, a cess pit? I've never smelled anything like that in my life, and I do include dead and rotting Army mules!"

Greenberg shrugged and said, "You gits used to it, after a time. Last patrol me and Rabbit-Boss led outten Havasu, we plumb forgot how them camels, and the whole outfit, stinks. We got payed off, went back down to Yuma, and spent nigh a week tryin' to figure

11

out why ever'body looked at us so funny. I took a real bath, with naptha soap and fresh-drawed water and, once I had most of it outten my hide, I wasn't able to put my duds back on. Had to buy me a whole new outfit and, even so, my boots and gunbelt smelled like camel shit fur about a month."

He spit over the rail and added, "Likely, that's one reason them camels ain't too popular with the U.S. Army, Jeff Davis or no."

Caldwell grimaced as he watched the mounted patrol lurch down the steep river bank and advance across the braided sandbars toward the steamboat. The closer they came, the less real they seemed. It was one thing to see pictures of camels in travel books, or even see them in the flesh behind the bars of a cage in the Philadelphia Zoo. A man expected to see weird beasts in a zoo. Right out in the open, like this, the massed camels took on a dreamlike quality. They belonged with the other mirages of the desert, at a respectful *distance!*

Down on the lower deck, Rabbit-Boss was shaking his digging stick at the camels and chanting something in his own language. Caldwell asked what the Indian was doing and Greenberg replied, "Takin' the bad medicine outten them. Old Rabbit-Boss don't allow as how them camels is real. Him and the other Injuns call 'em Spirit Horses and tell a tale about the Army Remount Service crossin' a buffalo with a mule or, mebbe, an antelope. I tolt the fool Injun how Jeff Davis got them critters offen the Turks, but, you see, Old Rabbit-Boss don't know no country but his own, and he allowed as how Jeff Davis was likely a heap bad Medicine Man. He says it ain't nachural to cross horses with burros to git a mule, but it's even worse to breed whatever in tarnation Jeff Davis bred to git them Spirit Horses."

Caldwell sighed and said, "Well, if I ever learn to ride one of those things, I ought to be able to scare the living daylights out of any Indians they send me out against. Who's this Diablito you were speaking of, before? I take it some of Rabbit-Boss' cousins have been getting out of hand?"

Greenberg laughed and said, "Diggers on the War Path? Not hardly, Lieutenant. Didn't they tell you nothin' back at Fort Yuma?"

Caldwell eyed the nearest camel morosely and, as its rider dipped his guidon in salute, muttered, "I'm afraid they left a lot out at my last briefing. If Diablito's not a Digger, who, or what, is he?"

Greenberg's voice was flat as he said, simply, "Apache. Diablito's band is Nedni-Apache, from south of the border. Betwixt you and me, Nedni-Apache is the worse kind. I mean, I've fit Mimbre-Apache, and Warm Spring-Apache, and none of 'em was all that neighborly. Next to them Mex-bred Nedni-Apache, though, our home-growed breed is a passel of schoolmarms. That Diablito jasper was just borned mean as hell and growed up larnin' to be even meaner. They do say he was runned outten Mexico by other Apache for bein' too loco fur even them to take."

He spit again and added, "I mean, you got to *study* bein' a Bad Injun, afore other Apache throws you out of the tribe!"

Caldwell stared at the color guard on the nearest camel and tried not to laugh as he returned the salute of the dipped guidon. It felt like he should be waking up, about now. Nobody in the War Department had ever intended to have a young man in U.S. Army Blue perched atop a camel's hump in the middle of the knee-deep Colorado, exchanging salutes in such a completely ridiculous way!

Staring in fascination at the supercilious leer on the approaching camel's split lips, Caldwell tried to cling to reality by saying to the scout at his side, "I don't understand this Apache business, Mister Greenberg. It was my understanding the Apache Nation is at peace with the U.S. Government at the moment. They also

13

told me, back East, that there are no Apache tribes west of the Colorado River."

Greenberg snorted and said, "You may understand that and the War Department may understand that, Lieutenant, but, you see, neither Old Diablito, nor any of the forty-odd braves in his renegade band read the *Army Journal* all that much."

The color guard with the guidon called out, "Captain Lodge's compliments, Sir. Would you be Lieutenant Caldwell?"

Matt Caldwell nodded as the other members of the patrol lined up their impossible mounts to face the rail. Another rider wearing the two gold stripes of a corporal reined in beside the color guard, or, rather, tried to as his camel slowly pirouetted in the shallow water to present its tail end to the steamboat. The corporal cursed, tried to swing his mount the right way, and then, as the camel lifted its tail and began to defecate what seemed to be a column of thick green pea soup, the red faced rider turned in his saddle to explain, "We've been sent to fetch you, Sir. What this lop-eared son of a bitch just done was its *own* idear!"

HALF A DAY's ride from the stranded steamboat, a short, heavy-set man sat cross-legged on the packed sand of a shallow wash, trying not to appear interested in the stranger whose shadow stretched across the sand in front of him. The stranger was a Nadene. No member of a lesser breed would have known where to find Kaya-Tenay and his people, let alone how to approach this close to thirty-seven Husbands and their people, alive. The stranger had come in on foot, giving the correct quail call just before the outlying pickets spotted him. He was standing there politely, waiting for Kaya-Tenay to notice him. But Kaya-Tenay was an important Husband, and the stranger was very young. There was a scar on one thigh that might have been left by a Papago arrow. Then again, the boy might have simply ridden too fast through chaparral and been speared by a mesquite limb. It was a thing worth asking about.

Kaya-Tenay said, "There is a scar on my shoulder that was made by a Mexican long knife. I do not boast of scars I got from riding my pony like a woman."

The stranger waited a moment before he answered. "This person was lanced in the thigh by a Pima on his fifth raid. The Pima does not speak of the matter, since he died shortly thereafter."

"A man who has ridden five times with honor may call himself a Husband."

"This person does. His name is Goyalka, and his people are the Nadene of the Warm Springs. He is a cousin, on his father's side, of a Nedni-Nadene Husband called Juh."

Kaya-Tenay nodded. "I knew the Husband called Juh in the Sierra Madre. He was not my enemy. You may speak to me in the first person if you are Juh's kinsman. My name, by the way, is Kaya-Tenay. The Mexicans call me Diablito for some reason."

Goyalka squatted down on his haunches and took a tobacco pouch from his medicine bundle. He began to stuff shredded tobacco in a turkey-bone pipe as he said softly, "I have come in peace with a message from Mangas Coloradas, Cochise, and Victorio, meeting in council with Noch-Ay-Del-Klinne and other Readers of the Dreams."

Kaya-Tenay studied some grains of sand on the ground in front of him and tried to think of a way to avoid what he knew was coming. Then he smiled and said, "Let us drink tiswin together before we speak of messages, Goyalka. Let us drink tiswin and tell each other of our first four raids, eh?"

The younger Husband said, "I mean no disrespect, almost-uncle, but Mangas Coloradas has forbidden me to drink with you. He says you have a bad thing inside your heart that comes out when you have had too much tiswin to drink. He says I am to deliver his message, and the message of the other leaders, while you are sober."

For the first time, Kaya-Tenay stared directly at the young Nadene who'd found his camp, unbidden. Goyalka was a stocky youth with a wide, thin-lipped mouth and piercing, unblinking, clear eyes. Kaya-Tenay glanced around at his followers, partly hidden in the brush half filling the dry-wash, and observed, "You are either very brave or very foolish, even for a distant kinsman, Goyalka. Did Mangas Coloradas say how you were to leave my rancheria alive after insulting me?"

The younger Husband shrugged and answered, "No. He only gave me a message for you. If you want to fight with me, I am willing, but I think it would be foolish for us to fight before you hear the words of my kinsmen."

Kaya-Tenay sniffed and said, "Speak, then. What is it Mangas Coloradas and the others wish for me to know?"

"They want you to know they are at peace with the White Eyes for the moment. A man named Butterfield has asked permission to carry words on paper through the White Mountains and down the Gila to California, and the Chiricahua have agreed to sell firewood to the American army. Our leaders think this is a bad time for you to be this far north with your people. The White Eyes are not as cruel as the Mexicans, but they too consider all Nadene except the ones they call Navajo to be one people. If you and your people take any horses or women up here, it will make trouble for Mangas Coloradas. He has asked me to tell you that if you get him in trouble he will dance in your blood."

Kaya-Tenay muttered, "I am not afraid of Mangas

Coloradas," and Goyalka smiled thinly as he kept what he was thinking behind his obsidian eyes. Kaya-Tenay protested, "My people and I are homeless refugees. The Mexican governor in Sonora has offered a reward for our scalps, and my women beg me not to expose them to such dangers."

Goyalka's voice was merciless as he said flatly, "You are not afraid of the Mexicans. No Mexican *soldado* could come within a day's ride of you in the Sierra Madre if your Nedni kinsmen were willing to have you among them."

"You accuse me of being an enemy to my people? You dare?"

"I accuse nothing. I speak the truth as it was told to me by my cousins from the south. You and these other Husbands were forced to leave the Sierra Madre because you drank too much tiswin and did a bad thing to Lozan, the daughter of Nana."

There was no word for rape in the Nadene language, but Goyalka's words dripped venomous contempt as he added, "The girl had not passed through her puberty rites, and even if she had, neither you nor the others who held her asked permission. They say you even tore her manta!"

"I did not hurt the teasing bitch, and besides, I was drunk. I offered Nana ponies for her maidenhead, but he said he would kill me the first time he found me alone. It was a misunderstanding, caused by too much tiswin in both our bellies, eh?"

"Nana is sober now, and he still wants to fight you. Why don't you go back to Mexico and face him like a man? Why are you and your people up here causing trouble for us with the White Eyes?"

"Listen, nephew, I am not a bad man, no matter what they say about me. We are not up here to make trouble. We just need a place to hide until Nana sells that slut of a daughter to someone and cools off, eh?"

Goyalka's jaw clenched, and for a moment he considered going for the throat of the older man, who'd just insulted the virtue of his second cousin Lozan, daughter of Nana. But the evil-tempered Kaya-Tenay was surrounded by at least thirty-seven Husbands, and heroism, while not unknown among Nadene, was considered somewhat foolish. So the youth Goyalka contented himself with saying, "There is no place on this side of the border where a man like you can hide without making trouble. There is no room for you in Nadene country, east of the Colorado. If you bring your people into our lands, we will fight you."

"And if I keep my people on this side of the river?"

Goyalka shrugged. "There is nothing here for a Real Person to live on. Unless you wish to live on crickets and rabbits, like the Paiutes, you must obtain food from the White Eyes, crossing the Big Emptiness. By the time the White Eyes' wagons come this far, they have little food and tobacco left to give or even sell."

"In that case, we shall *take* what we want from the passing White Eyes! What do you say to that, Husband of five raids?"

Goyalka got back to his feet and put away his tobacco. Mangas Coloradas and the others were right—Kaya-Tenay was a fool with some bad thing eating at his heart.

The younger Nadene said, "I think I am going away from this place. I think there will be many White-Eyed *soldados* here soon, and I am not of a mind to die today."

Kaya-Tenay called out to one of his women, "Cho-Ko-Ley! Bring tiswin! The mouthings of this babe are as the buzzing of a fly in my ears and all this talk has made me thirsty!"

Goyalka was moving away in the soft catlike walk of a trained Nadene Husband. He would soon vanish, as his people were taught to vanish on the trail in strange or unfriendly lands. Kaya-Tenay called after him, "Farewell, Woman Heart! Tell your grandmother, Mangas Coloradas, I am not going to frighten him by crossing into his country, eh?"

18

Goyalka ignored the jibe. He had a lot of distance to cover, and it seemed a waste of time to trade insults with a man who could not hold his tiswin. Breaking into a mile-eating dog trot, Goyalka told the angry voice of his insulted Dream Spirit, "There was not time to explain we were not what he took us for. Besides, it matters not what a Two-Heart thinks of one. Our friends know who we are. Yes, and our enemies, too! At the Battle of Arizpe, we taught the Mexicans we were more than a four-raid Husband. Heya! What was that name they gave us at Arizpe?"

Goyalka smiled wolfishly as he loped away from the camp of the man he considered a foolish, bloodthirsty idiot. He remembered the name the frightened Mexicans called him now.

It was Geronimo.

MOUNTING A CAMEL can be difficult at any time. Climbing aboard a cantankerous dromedary from the deck of a steamboat stranded in the middle of the muddy Colorado was an experience neither to be forgotten nor, if possible, repeated.

The idea seemed simple enough until one thought about it. The apple-cheeked corporal somehow got his dancing mount close enough to the steamboat to grasp the rail as he explained the form to Matt Caldwell. Meanwhile, another rider led a camel with an empty saddle up, pinned it against the steamboat with his own mount and a stream of odd sing-song curses, and grinned across at Caldwell in what might have been meaning to be a reassuring manner.

The corporal, whose name turned out to be Muller,

said, "High Jolly, here, will see you safe to the fort, sir. All you got to do is scrootch out across the rail into that saddle and hang on. Me and the others'll see to your baggage and sech.'"

Caldwell eyed the bobbing Turkish saddle on the other side of the rail dubiously. The top of the camel's hump came almost to the height of the rail, but the gap between it and the solid oak varied alarmingly as the animal these obvious lunatics expected him to mount tried to break free. The lithe young man called High Jolly kept a tight hold on the leather thong attached to a brass ring through the camel's pierced nose. The oddly named man was dressed in a rag-tag costume consisting of a cast-off army jacket, white cotton Mexican pants, and a flat topped Spanish sombrero worn over the red kerchief wrapped around his head. He seemed, at first glance, to be Mexican. At second glance, it wasn't too clear just what he was. High Jolly was a funny name for a Mexican, or anyone else, for that matter. When he said, "I have the thrice-accursed beast secure, if you would only mount her!" Caldwell wondered what sort of an accent that was. Could the civilian be some sort of . . . gypsy?

Caldwell realized he was stalling and, making the supreme effort, leaned out over the rail to grapple with the high pommel of the odd saddle, a thing that looked like a cross between a saw-horse and a cut-down rocking chair. Regulation U.S. Army stirrups had been fastened to the skimpy leather thongs and Caldwell had noticed, as High Jolly rode up, that the civilian cameleer rode barefoot with one big toe hooked through a brass ring on either side of his own rig. Caldwell had no idea the camels had come with Turkish saddles, of course, but he sensed that the little brass toe rings went more properly with the rest of the odd saddle.

Another soldier had led a second camel alongside for Digger Greenberg, and the scout, who'd done this sort of thing before, was climbing on the proffered mount as Caldwell was still trying to get up the nerve to try.

Despite High Jolly's reassuring smile, it seemed a hell of a way down between the steamboat rail and the bobbing saddle atop the skittish camel's ugly hump. Caldwell was not afraid of the six- or seven-foot fall because he thought it would kill him, rather he was thinking about what the men of his new command would whisper about a brand-new shavetail who took a full-dress pratfall into the muddy river.

He took a deep breath, put a toe into the planks of the railing, and swung his right leg desperately over and out, clinging for dear life to the high pommel.

It was well he did so. As his weight landed in the hard saddle, the camel belched, burbled, and tried to dance backward out from under him. High Jolly swore in an odd language, whacked the camel across the eyes with the free end of the leather lead, and gasped, "Hang on! I have the evil-tempered daughter of Shaitan, Effendi!"

Then, before Caldwell could answer, High Jolly screamed, *"arragh! Hike! Hike! Burrrro, Hike!"* as he allowed Caldwell's mount to lurch away from the steamboat rail. Caldwell gulped and hung on as the saddle under him pitched like a schooner in a full gale. Caldwell decided he wasn't going to fall off, after all, and risked a look back.

Behind him, Greenberg's camel followed, led by a blond soldier on another mount. The Indian, Rabbit-Boss, had simply leaped over the rail and was wading ashore under his own power. The water wasn't deep, and Caldwell could only envy the Digger's more sensible way of tagging along.

Corporal Muller and the others were climbing aboard the steamboat to get Caldwell's luggage and, if Caldwell knew his dragoons, a round of drinks at the steamboat's salon bar. He turned to High Jolly and asked, "Don't you think we should wait for the others?"

High Jolly answered, "But no, Effendi, my orders were to deliver yourself to the captain now, and, though Allah be more merciful, the captain is a man of temper!"

Caldwell shot the man at the other end of the camel lead a closer look. His accent was a curious mixture, between that of a Frenchman and . . . something else. His dark hatchet face and hawk-like nose made him seem more like Caldwell's idea of what a Jew should look like than did the broad features of Digger Greenberg, and—what was that he'd said about *Allah?*

Caldwell suddenly smiled and said, "You must be one of those Turkish drovers the army hired to take care of these camels, right?"

High Jolly said, "That was true in the beginning, Effendi, but, through the grace of Allah The Most High And Compassionate, Haji Ali is now an American, almost."

The trooper leading Greenberg's camel had drawn abreast of High Jolly, by this time, and the scout had caught the last part of their conversation. He called across to Caldwell, "High Jolly's carried on the payroll with civilian status, like me and the other white scouts. I don't savvy how in tarnation they figured him to be a white man, but he sure as hell aint no Injun, so I reckon it's all right."

He spit to the polite side of his camel and added, "Me and him has rode together afore. Don't let his funny ways spook you, Lieutenant. High Jolly looks like a prissified Mex and talks like he was raised in a whorehouse, but he's got enough sand in his craw to see him through in a pinch."

By this time they'd reached the bank, and Matt Caldwell couldn't talk, or even breathe, until the beast he rode lurched up the steep slope in a series of groaning, burbling staggers. The camel was much taller than a horse, and its hump seemed to flop from side to side in a sickening motion. Camels didn't walk like horses, cows, or any other sensible four-legged animal. A camel paced. The front and rear legs on either side moved forward together, making the camel's motion a series of lunges. He glanced down at the brush-covered ground, now that they were out of the river bed, and saw that despite the side-to-side motion they were moving forward at a respectable clip. A camel moved at what would be a slow trot for a horse or mule. Caldwell saw that Rabbit-Boss was jogging along on foot out to one side, and asked Greenberg, "Doesn't the Indian rate a ride?"

The scout laughed and said, "Shoot, you can't *git* a Digger to ride iffen he can help it. That's what makes him a Digger."

"Don't any of the desert tribes ride?"

"Well, sure they does. That's how you know a Digger from a Snake!"

Caldwell ran that through a few times before he shook his head and said, "Greenberg, I don't know what the hell you're talking about!"

The scout explained, "Diggers is Injuns that live out here on foot. Snakes is Injuns as have ponies. Didn't they tell you *nothin'* about the desert afore they sent you out here to replace that other jasper?"

"Not as much as they should have, I guess. I take it Snakes and Diggers are different tribes, eh?"

"You take it wrong, then. You put a Ute on a pony and he's calt a Bannock. Leave him on his own two feet and he's a calt a Paiute. Only that's jest white folks talkin'. The Injuns out this way don't know they's Utes, Paiutes, Bannocks, and sech. They mostly talk the same Shoshoni lingo hereabouts, and they got all sorts of names fer each band. The big difference betwixt the desert folks is the way they *live*. The Snakes live horseback. The Diggers don't."

"You mean Rabbit-Boss's people are superstitious about riding horses?"

"Not exactly. Horses jest don't go with the way Diggers live out here. You see, a man on foot kin go in parts of the desert a pony cain't. The Snakes have to keep close to hills and water. The Diggers go jest about anywhere they please, and Rabbit-Boss is one wanderin' son of a bitch. I never have got it straight jest where he was birthed out here in the basins and ranges. One time he tolt me he'd been to the Humboldt in the north and the Yaqui in the south by the time he was old enough to bed a squaw. I reckon that's why I keep him. Old Rabbit-Boss knows parts of this here country as ain't on no map yet."

Caldwell asked, "You say you keep him? I thought he was a scout hired like yourself by the army."

Greenberg laughed. "Shoot, nobody *hires* a Digger. They don't savvy what money is. You see that stick and medicine bundle he's totin' along there? That's all that muley old Injun owns in this world, and all he sets any value by."

"What about that antelope-horn headdress?"

"Oh, that's jest a fool notion he's been wearin' lately. He took it offen a Mojave who sassed him a few weeks back. It's a Mojave medicine man's headdress, and Rabbit-Boss wears it to piss them off. His folks don't cotton to Mojaves much."

"Why? They told me the Mojave were peaceful farmers along the Lower Colorado. What does Rabbit-Boss have against them?"

"Beats the shit outa me, Lieutenant. Injuns take funny notions on each other, which is jest as well fer *ussen*. I mean, you take the Crow and the Sioux, now. The Crow talk Sioux, dress Sioux, hunt buffalo like Sioux, and even pray to the same god, Wakan-Tonka. Yet ever' chance they git, them Crow and Sioux fight like cats and dogs. Do the Sioux rise

24

agin' the whites, them Crows jump right in with both feet and help the army and settlers whup 'em! Nobody's ever figured why, but it purely makes it easier to settle west of the Big Muddy, and that's the truth!"

Caldwell nodded, watching the effortless lope of Rabbit-Boss as he tried to keep his stomach under control. The odd gait of his mount was making him seasick. He took out another cigar and started to chew it unlit as he asked, to pass the time of day, "Are all the Diggers opposed to the Apache, too?"

"Can't rightly say. Each band sort of moseys about with the bit betwixt its own teeth. Pimas and Papagos hate Apache. Come to think of it, jest about ever'body hates Apache hereabouts."

"I guess they have good reasons. From what I hear, the Apache nation has done little to endear itself to its neighbors."

Greenberg said, "Well, they do like to raid more'n a good neighbor oughta. But it ain't jest that. You see, the Apaches is *strangers* in these parts. A Pueblo I talked to one time tolt me the Apaches only come down here to the Southwest about the time the Mexicans was comin' up from the south. Apaches, they calls themselves Nadenes, used to live up in Alaska Territory, where them Russians have the fur trade now. The lingo they talk is the same as Athapascan and them other Totem-pole tribes up north. The Pueblos say the Apache got run outten Alaska fer bein' too pi'zen mean fer the other Athapascans to stomach. They come down thisaway about the time Cortez was whuppin' the Aztecs, and the feudin' and fussin' ain't stopped since."

"Well, things will be different now that we've taken this country over from the Mexicans. I'm sure this Diablito is just a renegade. The other chiefs have made peace with Washington and . . ."

"Sonny, I mean, Matt, you got a heap of study ahead of you on Injuns, if you aim to keep your scalp long enough to retire with it!"

Before Caldwell could answer, High Jolly suddenly yelled, *"Adda! Adda!"* and the camel Caldwell was riding made a drunken stagger to one side. He saw the Turk had steered them around a clump of cactus. Caldwell asked, "Is that how you tell this thing to turn, High Jolly?"

The drover answered, "El Jamal is commanded by voice, Effendi, but whether one can *tell* the thrice-accursed creature anything is open to question. The ring in its nose reminds it to listen, for in truth, El Jamal considers kindness on a rider's part a sign of weakness and, though Allah be more merciful, El Jamal has no respect for anyone or anything it can take advantage of."

"How long do you think it will take me before I can control this camel on my own?"

"Inshallah, a few weeks, Effendi. You are a big man, and you do not look like a soft man. If you let me teach you, we shall know by the end of this month whether Allah fated you to ride El Jamal."

Caldwell looked back. They'd come a surprising distance from the steamboat, and he could see Corporal Muller and the others riding to catch up. He asked High Jolly, "Did you have much trouble teaching those other men how to ride these things?"

"Ah, those men, Effendi, were born with the kismet Allah bestows on one out of five. Of the men who joined the program in the beginning, only a handful were able to learn the art of the Mehari. You see, some were not strong enough. Others, too many others, were stronger than they needed to be. They were—how do you say it—muleskinners?"

"Most army men know something about whipping a mule into shape."

"Ah, but Effendi, El Jamal is not a mule. He is as stubborn as a mule, and at times more vicious. But he cannot be *treated* like a mule, *compris?*"

"If you mean, do I understand, I don't. You treat

26

a horse gently. You treat a mule more firmly. I'm completely in the dark about camels!"

"Ah, that is the beginning of wisdom, Effendi. Most of the troopers back at the remount station thought they *knew* about them! Some tried to ride them like horses, and of course, the camels laughed at them and scraped them off on the first gate they came to."

"And the others, the muleskinners?"

"They beat their mounts and yanked on the nose reins until the blood flowed red. I and the others from Izmir tried to stop them, but some men do not listen. It was very sad, and in the end we only had a few animals and riders worth keeping."

"What happened?"

"What my fellow drovers and myself said would happen, Effendi. Some of the abused camels killed their tormentors, first. But most of them merely died, as El Jamal is in the habit of doing when he feels unappreciated."

"You mean, most of the camels the War Department purchased for use in the western deserts never made it past the eastern remount stations?"

"Just so, Effendi. My poor Osmanli comrades fared little better and were sent home by the angry Americans. Myself and three or four others at other posts are all that remains of the original band."

Matt Caldwell knew the rough hazing the regulars dished out to any new recruit. Despite the officers' attempts to stop it, a good number of rookies in every new draft were driven to desertion, suicide, or murder by the brutality of basic training. The question wasn't what the roughneck troopers had done to haze High Jolly's Muslim comrades into quitting, but rather how the delicately built little Turk had stuck it out this far. High Jolly, Matt decided, had more sand in his crew than his appearance indicated.

Something fluttered in the heat haze ahead, and Caldwell realized it was the Stars and Stripes. Squinting against the deceptive glare, he could make out a long, low wall of adobe brick with a slightly higher watchtower near the open gate. The Muslim leading him in like a sack of supplies on a pack mule warned, "Hold onto the saddle cross, Effendi. There are Mojave children about, and by the breasts of Fatima, they are most miserable brats!"

Something whizzed by Caldwell's face and arched over into the blue-gray brush to his left. He gaped after it a moment before he blurted, "God damn it, that was an *arrow!*"

Digger Greenberg called softly, "Don't show as you notice, Matt," and Caldwell answered, "What are you talking about? Didn't you see that God damn thing just miss my nose?"

"They *always* miss when they's funnin', Matt. I got the little bastards spotted over yonder ahint that clump of pear. Couple of shitty Mojave kids teasin' us with quail arrows. Ain't no points on quail arrows, so . . ."

Another arrow snicked out from the clump of prickly pear and passed between Caldwell's chest and the head of his camel. The scout said, "What did I tell you? They ain't aimin' to hit you. But they got you singled out on account you paid attention to the first one."

Caldwell glanced over at the dog-trotting figure of Rabbit-Boss to see how the Indian was taking this new development. The Digger seemed oblivious as he jogged on, eyes on the fort ahead. A Mojave arrow hit Rabbit-Boss in the right thigh and bounced off and the naked Indian never broke stride. Caldwell said, "I thought you said they were aiming to miss!" and Greenberg explained. "They been tolt to miss *ussen.* Rabbit-Boss don't count. But, like I said, they's shootin' blunt ended quail arrows, so what the hell, it's all in fun."

"They make the animals uneasy," observed High Jolly. "If the captain would let me, I would teach these savages to behave!"

Greenberg shook his head. "They're behavin' neighborly enough, considerin'. I ain't sayin' Mojaves is friendly Injuns, you understand. They's sort of sulky about us movin' in and buildin' forts and sech along their river. But aside from lettin' their young'uns hoorah folks a mite, they ain't so bad."

High Jolly clicked his tongue and called out, *"Burrro, arrrah, hike, hike!"* and all four camels broke into a stiff-legged trot. The invisible Mojave youths were left behind out of arrow range as Rabbit-Boss picked up the pace with neither comment nor visible effort.

The new motion, coupled with the hot sun, made it impossible for Caldwell to do more than swallow the green taste in his mouth and hang on for dear life. The only ray of hope he saw in this ghastly ride from the river was that at this rate it would soon be over. The fort was much nearer now, and he had to admit a camel crossed a lot of country in a hurry. The animal he rode stood at least six feet at the shoulder. Higher yet, up here on the hump. Those long legs gave it nearly twice the stride of any horse, and if what they said about them going nine days between waterings was true, he could see certain advantages to Secretary Davis's wild-sounding scheme. If, as Greenberg said, the Horse Indians were confined to the greener, more watered parts of the desert, a fighting Camel Corps seemed just the thing to police the Great American Desert.

If only, he added with a groan, somebody could teach the goddamn things to move in a straight line like reasonable animals!

CHO-KO-LEY HAD NEVER been beautiful, even in her
youth, but she was a strong woman and, in the darkness of a wickiup, a warm-thighed woman who knew
how to pleasure a man better than many a younger,
slimmer wife.

But Cho-Ko-Ley was not lying naked between her
deerskin robes now, and the afternoon sun etched
cruel lines across her broad brown face as she scooped
a hole in the drywash sand with her work-hardened
fingers. Cho-Ko-Ley's face was passive, but her heart
beat wildly inside her breast as she dug, for she knew
the thing she planned was a terrible sin. No woman
of her clan had ever disobeyed a Husband as far as
Cho-Ko-Ley knew, and at her puberty rites many seasons ago the horrors that awaited a disobedient wife in
the Long Sleep had been drummed into her together
with the two hundred and fifty names of the two hundred and fifty Nadene gods!

Cho-Ko-Ley glanced around and saw she seemed to
be unobserved by the others, hiding in the dry-wash
from the eyes of distant strangers. She slid the leather
tiswin bottle inside her skirt and moved forward to
crouch over the hole she'd scooped in the sand. If any
one saw her, they'd think she was relieving herself in
the usual manner.

Gripping the tiswin bottle between her thighs, Cho-
Ko-Ley reached under herself and pulled the corncob
stopper. The home-brewed mixture of mescal and
corn liquor gushed out, and Cho-Ko-Ley giggled as she
thought, "Such a pissing would do honor to a pony!"

And then her secret Spirit Voice whispered, "Do

not laugh! You have just done a terrible thing! You have just poured your Husband's last bottle into the earth!"

Cho-Ko-Ley moved off the latrine hole and quickly scooped sand onto the spilled liquor as she muttered to herself. "I did it to save him from the bad thing inside his heart. I did it for the man Kaya-Tenay used to be."

She put the empty bottle aside and smoothed the sand over the scene of her crime. The sand was warm and felt as clean and sensuous as a new deerskin against Cho-Ko-Ley's once young hands. The cruel daylight illuminated the jagged white scar on the woman's left forearm, but Cho-Ko-Ley ignored the place her man had struck at her with the knife. He'd been too drunk to really hurt her, after all, and it wasn't as if it had been Kaya-Tenay's fault. Everyone knew there was something bad inside his heart. Something that came out when he drank too much tiswin.

There was no tiswin now. The band was far from the Sierra Madre, in a strange, flat place Cho-Ko-Ley could not name. Her Husband said the hand of every man was turned against them in this place, and Cho-Ko-Ley was glad. If Kaya-Tenay had no friends in this new land, them perhaps he could not get drunk here, and perhaps things could be as they'd been so long ago, when Kaya-Tenay's stomach was still flat and one fierce, loving wife had been enough for him!

A shadow fell across the sand where Cho-Ko-Ley could see it. It was the shadow of a friend, for no Nadene cast a shadow where an enemy could see it, and no one else could move up behind one so silently.

Cho-Ko-Ley said, "This person was shitting. She hopes she was not shamed by another's eyes at such a time."

A young man's voice said, "Mother, it is me." The woman nodded. "I knew it was you, Eskinya. Only

31

a son I helped to teach could move so like a puma through this dry brush!"

The youth dropped to his haunches at his mother's side with a pleased blush. He knew his mother flattered him and he knew it was wrong to feel pride in the idle prattle of a mere woman, but his mother was a good person, and though Eskinya had no word that would describe love as a white son might mean it, he loved his mother just the same.

There was a smell of tiswin about his mother, and Eskinya knew she did not drink. He noticed the empty bottle and guessed at once what this might mean. Looking away, Eskinya said, "I was to the north just now, scouting for sign. I went far, but I kept low and nothing saw me. I thought once a buzzard had noticed me in the brush, but I made signs at it and it flew on."

"One must signal a buzzard that one still lives, lest it start to circle and give your position away," nodded the woman. They were just making conversation, she knew. The tricks of hiding on the trail were taught to all Nadene from birth.

Eskinya sighed and said, "I came across the track of a White Eye's wagon. There is a wagon trace not far north from here. I read in the pebbles that many wagons have passed from the east to west there. Only one, however, has passed within the past few days."

The woman didn't answer, and Eskinya flushed as he explained, "I did not guess at this thing, Mother. There were fresh horse droppings and in one place freshly crushed greasewood. The leaflets had not fallen from the broken twigs and . . ."

"I know you read signs," his mother cut in gently. "Get to the thing that troubles you, my son."

Eskinya said, "One wagon, alone, not far. I think if I tell my father and the others, they will want to go after it. The sign reads no more than two men. Maybe women riding the wagon, but only two men."

"How many horses?"

"Four. But I think they are mules. The shoe prints

were like those shoes the Mexicans put on mules for the White Eyes over in the Gila Valley. I think two men are striking out across the desert alone, looking for the Yellow Iron the White Eyes like so much. I think if I tell the others, it will be a saguaro fruit they won't be able to resist plucking!"

"Then what are you waiting for? Why don't you tell your father what you know?"

Eskinya stared down at the sand. "I have been thinking of what that Husband who just visited us said. I have been thinking that our brothers will be angry if we stir the Blue Sleeves up by going after those White Eyes and their wagon."

"The messenger of our northern cousins has gone away to lick the boots of his White-Eye'd masters. Mangas Coloradas has no way of knowing what we do, as long as we do it over here on this side of the Great Red River."

"He will know, Mother. Mangas Coloradas sits like a spider in a web, listening and watching to what goes on about his people. They say he does not trust the White Eyes. They say he does not trust Cochise. They say he does not trust anyone. He just sits and waits, until he makes up his heart. I think Mangas Coloradas has two hearts. I think he could turn against the White Eyes, or against us. I think it would be foolish to irritate him."

Cho-Ko-Ley nodded, watching a small green fly as it crawled across the wetness of the corncob stopper she'd forgotten on the sand. Her son was wise for his years. Her words would have to make sense to him. Therefore they would have to be chosen carefully.

Cho-Ko-Ley said, "I am only a woman, but I have lived longer than many of the Husbands in this band. I have lived through many War Walks following my Husband with the spare ponies and more than once carrying him from the field to tend his wounds. Once when the Mexicans had your father pinned down in an arroyo, I slipped above them onto the rimrocks, and three of them died before the others ran away. Another time the Papagos came to our rancheria while the Husbands were away. The other wives screamed. I killed the Papago leader with my bare hands, and when the other wives took heart and joined me, the Papagos learned to their sorrow that a Nadene born a woman was still, by the two hundred and fifty gods, a *Nadene!*"

"These things are known to me, Mother. I have heard my father say that had you been born a man, you would have been as great a Husband as himself. Once when he was sick from too much tiswin, he wept and said he had wished many times for a brother such as yourself. In truth, you are wise and strong for a woman, but your words puzzle me. I think there is something you want to say, but you hesitate to say it for some reason."

Cho-Ko-Ley nodded. "I do not know how to speak like a Husband, even to my son. But my thoughts are not the thoughts of a wife."

"What are these thoughts, my mother?"

"They are about the wagon tracks you found out there. You say they lead west away from the river."

"That is true. The White Eyes are alone on the desert, at least a day's walk into the sunset."

"They will be moving slowly, as White Eyes move with their many possessions and soft, grain-fed ponies. It would be easy for us to catch up with them. Two men with rifles would mean nothing to you and the others. I think it would be a good fight."

Eskinya looked away, shocked by his mother's boldness. A sexual advance from her could hardly have confused him more, for Nadene women did not suggest a fight. They had the right, if one of their men had been killed, to demand vengeance, and such torturing of prisoners as the Nadene went in for was usually done by bereaved widows and sisters of the fallen. Initiating action against an enemy, by a woman, was unheard of. Perhaps, he thought, his mother *had* been drinking the tiswin he still smelled in the dry heat of the wash!

Cautiously, Eskinya asked, "Do you know the White Eyes with the wagon, Mother? Have the spirits granted you a vision of some old enemy among the seekers of Yellow Iron?"

Cho-Ko-Ley said, "No. I care nothing about the people crossing the desert to the northwest."

"You wish to possess their rifles or their ponies or the things White Eyes carry in their heavy wagons?"

"I wish nothing they have. I only want your father to lead us after them away from the river."

Eskinya frowned, trying to understand. His mother was staring strangely at a little green fly on a corncob near her knees. Eskinya watched the fly for a moment. Then his hand moved with the swiftness of a striking sidewinder, and the fly was buzzing unharmed inside Eskinya's closed fist. He said, "If this fly was bothering you, I will kill it." But his mother said, "Let it go. It is bad to kill anything that lives without reason."

Eskinya opened his hand, allowing the fly to escape. Then he asked quietly, "Do we have a reason to kill the people with the wagon?"

Cho-Ko-Ley nodded. "Yes. It will take our band a day's travel to the west away from the river, and away from anywhere we can obtain freshly brewed tiswin."

Eskinya's eyes hardened in understanding. His mother suddenly buried her face in her hands. Then Eskinya said soberly, "I think I will tell the others about the wagon. I will try to catch the wagon before the others, and if there is White Eyes' tiswin in the wagon in one of those brown glass bottles, I will break it before I do anything else. I will kill the White Eyes and break all their bottles."

Cho-Ko-Ley fought for self-control as she husked, "You've always been a good boy, Eskinya!"

"ALL RIGHT, MISTER, what are you, a thief, a drunk, or a damn fool Abolitionist?"

Matt Caldwell stood at attention in the Fort Havasu orderly room as he wondered just how he was supposed to answer his new commanding officer. Captain Calvin Lodge was a prim-lipped man of forty-odd, with thinning gray hair and a Yankee whaler's chin whiskers. He was seated behind an improvised desk of unplaned lumber as he stared unwinkingly up at his new junior officer. The room was stuffy and dark despite the whitewash on the adobe walls. A faded, tattered flag was pinned to the rear wall, beside a large tan paper map, too lightly drawn to make out from where Matt stood. The captain asked, "Well?" and Matt replied, "The captain has my service record and orders in front of him."

Lodge glanced down and snorted, "They even spelled *camel* wrong. It says you were stationed at Leavenworth before they sent you out here. You didn't notice whether the Free-Staters or Southern guerillas were winning back in bleeding Kansas, did you, Mister?"

"I'd say it was about a draw, sir. Last summer the Slavocrats burned Lawrence nearly off the map. Then John Brown and the Free-Staters hit at Pottawatamie and murdered three Southerons. As fast as we could round them up, the local courts just turned them loose."

"You rode against both sides?"

"Tried to, sir. Our orders were to shoot John

Brown's men on sight, but he rode out of the state before we could catch him."

"What about the others, the pro-slavery guerillas?"

Matt Caldwell didn't answer. His commander at Leavenworth had been a Virginian. Captain Lodge would know that, if he'd really read the transfer papers.

Lodge nodded grimly and asked, "What did you do, son, write a letter over your captain's head?"

Matt shook his head and said, "No, sir. I was taught to always go through channels."

"In other words, you protested formally against the way the army's been favoring the Slavocrats in Kansas."

It was a statement, not a question, so Caldwell didn't answer. Captain Lodge got up and went to a campaign chest on a side table. He took out a bottle and two thick glass tumblers and came back to the desk. He poured two drinks. "Welcome to Fort Havasu, Lieutenant. It's hard to find our kind of people in this man's army since that piss-ant Jeff Davis got control of it!"

Matt Caldwell picked up his glass, but held it untasted as he said, "Sir, I believe it's my duty to inform you I am not an Abolitionist."

Lodge cocked an eyebrow. "No? What are you, then?"

"A *soldier,* sir. I don't consider it a soldier's duty to take sides in a political argument."

"But you got in trouble back in Kansas by protesting your former C.O.'s pro-slavery views."

"I didn't protest his views, sir. I protested his dereliction of duty. Our job at Leavenworth was to keep order in Kansas. I didn't consider it our duty to look the other way when either side burned a barn or a town. I mean, had my C.O. been favoring the Free-Staters against the Southerons, I'd have protested *that,* too!"

Lodge laughed bitterly. "That'll be the day, when

Jeff Davis allows anyone but a Slavocrat sympathizer to command a vital post. Don't you see what's happening, Mister? For God's sake, he just made Robert E. Lee the commandant at West Point!"

"I'm afraid I don't know Colonel Lee, sir. I understand he's a good soldier. Wasn't he one of the captains who took Mexico City in the last war?"

"He was, and so was I, along with a pretty fair fighter named U.S. Grant. We were all captains then, Mister. Only, Sam Grant's been driven out of the army on trumped-up drinking charges and I . . . I'm still a captain at a frontier post too far west to matter. Yet Bobby Lee's a colonel in command of the most strategic post in the Union. It makes you wonder, doesn't it?"

"I'm not sure just what you're suggesting, sir."

"I daresay you don't read the newspapers, then. Haven't you been following the Lincoln–Douglas debates, Mister?"

Caldwell shrugged and replied. "Not too closely, sir. It's my understanding that backwoods lawyer, Lincoln, is just out for some public notoriety at the expense of Senator Douglas and the Moderates."

"That backwoods lawyer's liable to be our next president, Mister! How do you feel about *that?*"

"I don't know why I'm supposed to feel *anything* about that, sir. If the voters elect this Lincoln fellow, I suppose we'll just have to live with whatever changes he wants in the War Department."

"You agree, then, that the President of these United States is your commander-in-chief?"

"Of course, sir. It says so right in the A.R.'s."

"I know what it says in the A.R.'s, Mister. But certain officers in this man's army have taken the position that they only have to obey a government they agree with in every way. How do you feel about that, Mister?"

"I feel that's wrong, if not high treason."

"Even if many of your superior officers or, say the

Secretary of War, were to tell you the new administration was being run by, well, a nigger-loving baboon?"

Caldwell met the other's stare levelly. "Sir, if the voters of the United States elect one of those camels there and it's able to give me an order, I guess I'll just have to try and carry it out."

Captain Lodge suddenly smiled, raised his glass, and said, "Drink your bourbon, son. You and me are going to get along just fine."

THE LATE AFTERNOON sun was low in the west, but still a white-hot ball in a sky of burnished brass. The man on foot leading the mule team trudged head down, shielding his eyes with the wide brim of his Mexican sombrero. The only other man in the party rode the tailgate of the lightly built prairie schooner, his eyes resting on the eastern horizon. A loaded Sharpe's rifle lay across his knees as his worn boots dangled above the California Trail. In the wagon, shaded but half stifled by the canvas cover, a feverish little boy moaned in his sleep as his worried mother held his head in her lap. Ernestine Unger was worried about more than her Willy's fever. She was on her way to join her husband at Los Angeles City, accompanied by her two children, black maid-servant, and two young men she'd hired in Santa Fe to tend the team, guard them from the savage men, both red and white, along the trail, and do such campsite chores as men were expected to do, moving west.

It had all seemed so simple back at Santa Fe. Her Hansel had sent her more than enough to buy and equip a good wagon. Hansel had a store near the beautiful Los Angeles River, and he wrote that the ranches and prospectors in California were stripping his shelves as fast as the clippers could deliver goods around the Horn. She'd paid more than she'd intended for the mules, but in truth, they were good mules and the Mexican who'd sold them to her had been more honest than he'd looked.

The wagon, too, had held up better than she'd expected, once she saw the mountains between the Rio Grande and Gila. She'd been about to purchase a heavy Conestoga for the trip, after traveling by stage as far as Santa Fe, but a nice ranchero, riding the last leg of the Santa Fe with her and the children, had warned her to travel light. And despite its frail-looking construction, the little prairie schooner had survived Apache Pass and the awful route down the Gila Valley.

Her servant girl, Jezebel, had been a dear on the long, hot journey, and the children, before this mysterious fever of Willy's, had been as well behaved as any mother can expect from an eight-year-old boy and a fourteen-year-old girl.

It was the young men she'd hired who were starting to worry her. The Mexican boy, Ramon, had never had much to say, but the last few days, his normal silence had turned to something else. Something more ominous than shy silence, or even sullenness. He was leading the team willingly enough at the moment, but, last night, when she'd asked him to fetch more firewood, he'd said something in Spanish and simply turned his back on her. Jezebel, in the end, had gone up the draw and found some dead mesquite.

Freddy Dodd, the other boy she'd hired in Santa Fe, had seemed a cheerful, smiling type in the beginning, but he, too, had taken to sulking the past few days. He was sulking even now, sitting with his back to them on the tailgate. Ernestine had asked him more than once what he and Ramon were unhappy about.

But Freddy had only looked away and answered, "Nuthin'," in an adenoidal whine she hadn't noticed in his voice before she'd listened to it all these weary days and nights along the California Trail.

Willy Unger moaned and rolled his head in Ernestine's lap. She turned to the Negress, closer to the rear, and whispered, "You'd best wet a towel for his head, Jezebel."

Jezebel reached for a keg near Freddy Dodd's right hip and the youth put a hand on it, saying, "You just leave the water be, she-coon! We ain't got water to waste on no wet towel hereabouts."

The black girl shot her mistress an inquiring look and Ernestine said, "He's burning up with fever, Freddy. A few drops of water on a towel might help to cool his head."

Freddy didn't look back as he spoke up. "A few drops of water might be worth a killin' two or three days further out. We're headed into the *Mojave,* lady! Do we strike water fit to drink this side of the Chuckawalla Range, it'll be worth puttin' on the map! We ain't got water to put on no towels. We ain't got water fer nothin' but drinkin', and if you aim to git across this time of the year, you'll let the mules drink first!"

Jezebel leaned back, unsure, holding a folded cotton cloth in her lap. Then Willy moaned again, licked his dry lips, and murmured, "Momma, make them let go my toes."

Ernestine hesitated, aware they were heading for the confrontation she dreaded. She knew that the sullen youth was an employee and that the water kegs, and everything else in the wagon, belonged to her. Yet, Freddy had said he knew the way to Los Angeles City, and this desert did seem awfully wide, so . . .

Willy's sister, Alfrieda, suddenly sat up where she'd been reclining near the front of the wagon bed and, crawling over her mother and feverish little brother, joined Jezebel in the rear. Alfrieda took the cotton cloth from the young Negress. "Here, I'll do it, fraidy cat!"

The girl started to tip the keg, ignoring Freddy's hand on it until he tried to resist her, then she slapped it away as she insisted, "You mind your manners, Freddy Dodd! You heard my momma say she wants a damp cloth for Willy."

Freddy half turned to glare at her, snapping, "God damn it, missy! I said not to trifle with that water and I mean it!"

Alfrieda stuck out her tongue. "Pooh! What are you going to do, hit me?"

Freddy looked confused. Alfrieda laughed, throwing her blond head back with a look more knowing than one might expect in a fourteen-year-old as she challenged, "Go on, I dare you, double dare you! You been wantin' to hit me ever since we started out, but you're a fraidy cat, ain't you?"

Freddy said, "Aw, shoot!" and turned away. Ernestine Unger murmured, "That's enough, Frieda," but the girl prattled on as she wet the cloth with a generous splash of tepid water. She said, "Well, it's true, I'll betcha. I've seen the way Freddy looks at me when he thinks I ain't lookin' back. He looks like he's just pinin' to give me a good lickin', but he ain't got the sand in his craw to try, so there!"

Ernestine took the damp cloth her daughter handed over and placed it gently on Willy's head. It was obviously time she and her budding daughter had a woman-to-woman talk about certain facts of life. Why, it seemed only yesterday that her Frieda was a pink and blond baby! Where had the years flown? *She* certainly didn't feel any older. Yet, suddenly men were looking at her little Frieda the way men looked at, for heaven's sake, a *woman!*

Frieda poked Freddy Dodd's elbow with a finger and asked, "What you lookin' at back there, Freddy? Ain't nothin' back that way but miles and miles of nothin' I ever want to see again!"

The youth muttered something and dropped to the ground behind the slowly moving wagon, the back of his neck red with confused emotions. He cradled the rifle in his right arm, finger on the trigger, and jogged around to the front to join his Mexican friend, plodding along beside the mules.

Freddy said, "I'll spell you a mite, if you want." But Ramon held on the leadline and said, "I am not tired, and the mules do not like it when you lead them. You do not have the touch for coaxing a weary mule, or a virgin, for that matter."

Freddy snapped, "Now, what's that supposed to mean, you mescal-soaked greaser? I guess I've handled as many mules, and women, too, as your ownself!"

Ramon shrugged and asked, "Is that why we are taking so much time with this business, then? You know we should have finished them off back there in Apacheria on the other side of the river, but, no, you keep saying, just one more night, one more night, one more night! By the Mother of God, I think you've lost your nerve!"

"I ain't lost my nerve. I just thought it'd be best to git them out in the wide open desert a ways first. You know I'da done 'em that one night back along the Gila, had not that derned old prospector come along and jined us at the fire!"

Ramon didn't answer. The two young owl-hoots trudged along for a time, hat brims lowered against the sun's baleful glare. Then Freddy said, "That derned old Frieda purely deserves what she's a-gonna *git,* you know that?"

Ramon said, "I think you want to lay with her. I think you waste all this time because you hope some way to make her give herself to you of her own free will." He sighed and added, "You know, of course, you are a fool."

"Shoot, I don't want that skinny little thing's old

cherry. Why, I'll bet she don't even know why boys and girls is different!"

"Then what are we waiting for? You know there is not enough food and water back there in the wagon for all six of us to reach the far side. The longer you take to make up your mind, the less reason there will be for us to kill them. They are swilling food and water like we were somewhere in the Land of Milk and Honey. At the rate we are going, none of us will reach California!"

Freddy Dodd nodded. "That's the truth, *amigo,* but, listen, I been thinkin' . . ."

"Thinking is a dangerous game for a man with no brains, *amigo.*"

"I guess I'm as smart as any dern murderin' Mexican, damn it! I guess I know how to reach California with the Ungers' money *and* a bit of fun!"

"Fun? What is this nonsense about fun, *amigo?* We agreed when we took this job it was an easy way to reach the gold fields with a grubstake. I do not remember anything about it being fun!"

"Well, listen, I been thinkin', if we jest kilt the old lady, the coon, and the puley little boy, there'd be enough water to keep old Frieda goin' fer a day or so."

Ramon plodded on, making disgusted noises deep in his throat, as Freddy insisted, "I'll share her with you, Ramon. I jest want to see her one time stripped down with all the sass scared outten her. I mean, I know we dasn't take her *all* the way with us alive, but what's to stop us from totin' her along fer a spell? She don't weigh all that much, and it ain't as if we'd have to feed or water her, once we had her trussed up right."

Ramon snorted in disgust. "I thought you didn't want the girl. It seems to me I just heard something about her being a skinny little thing."

Freddy Dodd grinned sheepishly. "Aw, what the hell, you know I been jerkin' off over her all the way across the mountains. I jest want to have her fer a little while, Ramon. Shoot, I'll even share her with you, afore we do her like her momma and the black gal."

Ramon didn't answer. He knew his companion too well to think he could talk him out of the thing he had in mind. Freddy was a lot like one of the mules he led. One could not yank the foolish gringo to one side, once he'd taken the bit in his teeth. One could but steer him gently in a more prudent direction.

Ramon said, "We shall be stopping for the night soon. We are nearly in the middle of this particular playa, and once it gets dark, nobody will ever know what we might choose to do out here between the ridges."

"What are you gettin' at, Ramon?"

"I am getting at both of us having our own way. I am getting at doing what must be done tonight. Do you have that cap-and-ball six-shooter that we took from the Texan loaded and primed?"

"Sure, it's in my bedroll back in the wagon."

"Good. This is what I want you to do. I want you to wait until we stop at sunset. Then I want you to slip the six-shooter to me and go off into the chaparral to gather firewood."

"Then what?"

"Then I intend to shoot the two women and, if he has not died of the cholera by nightfall, the sick *muchacho*. The virgin I shall save for you. We shall build no fire, and while I stand guard, you will get this nonsense about her out of your system."

"Hot damn! You're gonna let me carry her along a spell?"

"No. Her body must be found with the others, tied to the wagon wheels and mutilated in Apache fashion. One night should be enough to teach you how little pleasure there is in an unwilling virgin,

45

and by sunrise we will be on our way, riding the mules, with the money, food, and water."

Freddy walked on in silence for a time before he said, "Well, I'll tell you what, I'll let you kill her in the mornin' if she still acts uppity. Mebbe, if she knows her life depends on it, old Frieda'll larn to treat me right and we won't have to kill her—all right?"

Ramon started to object, then nodded and said, "As you wish, *amigo.*" Freddy muttered, "Hot damn! I can hardly wait for that old sun-ball to go down!" and Ramon sighed in genuine sorrow for his poor, foolish former *companero* and the postponement of his trip to the gold fields of California.

There was no point in further talk or another wasted day on the trail to nowhere. A man needed to eat, a man needed to drink, and a man needed to womanize, but if he was a real man, he satisfied his needs when they did not get in the way of his common sense. This gringo at his side was not a man. He was a whimpering boy, begging like a baby for a piece of candy; and a prudent man did not try to cross a hundred and fifty miles of basin and range in August with a baby!

Freddy was saying, "I don't see why you want me to go off when it's time to do 'em, Ramon. I mean, I kin shoot the nigger whilst you shoot the mother and we'll flip to see who gits to do the kid."

Ramon shook his head. "No. It is better my way. You will give me the gun when we stop, and I will shoot everyone. Then I will leave Apache sign, and if anyone ever finds them . . ."

"Yeah, but you jest remember I git a night with old Frieda afore we do *her,* right?"

"Es verdad," Ramon shrugged, promising. "You shall spend the night in the wagon wih her. You have my word."

He saw no reason to add that Freddy would be dead when he burned them side by side in the wagon.

There were six rounds in that pistol. He'd shoot
Freddy point-blank as the gringo handed it to him
that evening. Then he'd shoot the Negress, the
mother, and the two children, in that order. He was
only a day's ride west of the Colorado. He'd ride back
on one mule with the Ungers' money and find himself a sensible partner before he headed once again
for the gold fields of California.

THE MOJAVE CAME in just after supper. He was alone
and on foot, and the corporal of the guard told the
two troopers who'd stopped the Indian at the gate
to take him to the captain. Captain Lodge, in turn,
told one of the troopers to stand by and sent the
other to fetch his scouts and junior officers. Then he
offered the Mojave a cigar and a seat in the orderly
room. The Mojave refused both and stood there silently, as the captain wondered what one said to a
visiting Indian who didn't seem to want anything.

The Mojave was a middle-aged man with a moonface and a thick waist. Like most tribesmen along
the Lower Colorado, he wore little more than a deerskin loincloth and yucca-fiber sandals. He carried
no weapon and seemed, after not receiving an answer to his first guttural words to the captain, to have
dozed off on his feet. His eyes were half closed,
and he ignored Lodge when the captain tried a few
words of Border Mex on him. After what seemed a
very long and awkward time, Digger Greenberg came
in with Rabbit-Boss. The Mojave frowned slightly and
asked Rabbit-Boss, "*I ne ma Mo-Ha-Vey?*"

Rabbit-Boss grunted, "*Ka!*" and squatted on the

floor near the door, not deigning to take further notice of the stranger. The captain shot Greenberg a puzzled look and the scout laughed and explained, "This old boy just asked Rabbit-Boss was he Mojave and Rabbit-Boss set him straight. I reckon them antelope horns puzzled the old geezer."

Lodge asked, "Can you speak Mojave, too?"

Greenberg shrugged and said, "Some. Mojave is a lot like Sioux. I'll be blamed if I kin figure how a mess of Sioux wound up as farmers on the Lower Colorado, but there you are. What do you want me to say to the varmint, Captain?"

"Ask him what he wants, for openers."

Greenberg nodded and began to address the Mojave in his own version of Lakota. The Mojave looked pained and said in English, "You talk funny. I can hardly understand half of what you are trying to say in my tongue. I think we should speak in yours."

Lodge gaped at the blank-faced Indian and asked, "Do you speak English, for God's sake? Why in thunder didn't you say so?"

The Mojave didn't answer.

Digger Greenberg said, "I've run across this dodge afore, Captain. Sometimes a man kin learn a mite by lettin' on he don't know what folks is sayin' about him."

Lodge nodded and, turning to the Mojave, said, "All right, my friend, you've had your little joke. Do you want to tell us what's on your mind, or do you want to stand there playing cigar-store Indian until someone carves their initials on you?"

The Mojave gave no indication whether he understood the sarcasm or not. He said, "I am called Owns-the-Water. My people farm an arroyo one day's walk from this place."

Lodge asked, "Upstream or down?" But Owns-the-Water ignored the question and said, "Some Apache think we did not see them cross the Mi-Ney-

Tonka, but we did. For the past few days, they think they have been hidden in a brush-filled dry-wash. My people have been watching them. There are thirty-seven men and forty-eight women in the band. They have seventeen children, sixty-four ponies, and eight burros. We have not finished counting their guns."

Lodge nodded soberly. "That sounds like Diablito's band. You say they're definitely on the west side of the . . . what did you call it?"

Greenberg cut in. "He meant the Colorado, Captain. He calt it the Great Water." Greenberg turned to the Indian and asked, "How far across your Mi-Ney-Tonka is the Apache camp, Owns-the-Water?"

The Mojave said, "One day south. One sunrise to high-noon west. I count this as my people travel."

Lodge shot the scout a puzzled look, and Greenberg said, "I make it thirty-odd miles south-south-west, Captain. Mojave make better time than a wagon train, less than Diggers or cavalry."

Lodge went over to the wall map, stabbed it with a finger, and mused, "Say it's somewhere about in *here*, it doesn't make much sense. There's nothing in that area but flat, dry scrub. What sort of hunting would there be in that sort of country, Greenberg?"

"Grasshoppers, mebbe. Late summer runs most critters offen the flats and into broken country. Small game hugs the washes and arroyos, this time of the Big Dry. Bighorns, deer, and pronghorn keep to the higher slopes of the desert ranges until the fall rains green the flats."

"They're pretty far south of the Immigrant Trail. They don't seem to be in a position to bother anyone."

Greenberg shook his head. "That's where you're wrong, Cap. They're botherin' the shit outten this here Mojave, or he'd have stayed put in his squash patch down that way. There's a sometimes wagon trace called Slocum's Cut-off runnin' past them patches betwixt the river and where it jines the main route further out to the west. You cain't cross the Colorado down that way when it's high water, but right about now a greenhorn could ford the danged crick anywheres!"

"You think they could be stalking a wagon train? No immigrants are supposed to set out across the open desert without checking in with us first."

"Lots of folks don't do as they're supposed to hereabouts, Cap." The Mojave hesitated, then cleared his throat and said, "Two men, two women, two children, one wagon. They did not see us as they went past. I think they have passed the Apache, too. If the Apache did not see them."

"Did your scouts hear any shots, Owns-the-Water?"

The Indian didn't answer. Foolish questions did not deserve an answer.

Greenberg explained, "He'd have said so if they had, Cap. Besides, no Apache's about to waste no shots snappin' up easy pickin's like that. If they've spotted them fool immigrants, by now it's all over."

Matt Caldwell came in, his face flushed, and said, "Sorry I'm late, sir."

Lodge asked, "Where's Lieutenant Gordon, Mister?"

"I don't know, sir. I've been trying to find him, but he's not in his quarters and . . ."

"Never mind. I told you they sent me nothing but thieves, drunks, and Abolitionists. Let me bring you up to date on what this Indian just came in with."

Caldwell studied the Mojave as he listened to his C.O.'s assessment of the situation. He noticed Rabbit-Boss glowering at the Mojave from his squatting place by the doorway. The Mojave was pretending a trifle obviously that Rabbit-Boss did not exist. When Captain Lodge asked, "Any questions, Mister?" Caldwell nodded and answered, "Yes, sir. I've been wondering why Mr. Owns-the-Water here is so anxious to betray the position of those other Indians."

Digger Greenberg snorted in disbelief. "Do Jesus, Lieutenant, didn't you jest hear the captain tell you that band was *Apache?*"

"You mean, *every* other tribe in the area is against them?"

"They is iffen they has women, ponies, or anything else worth stealin'. Diablito's band, if that's the outfit holed up down there, is short at least two dozen mounts. Most of the women and kids is ridin' double, and by now the whole bunch is hungry. There ain't enough to feed a band of Diggers in that neck of the desert, and Diggers run in small bands and don't eat all that much. This hombre, Owns-the-Water, don't cotton all that much to havin' Apache neighbors, even iffen Diablito don't know about it. I mean, like I said, the Mojaves are some breed of long-lost Sioux, halfways to becoming Pueblos, and they still keep more ponies than most farmin' tribes."

Matt Caldwell nodded in sudden understanding and, smiling at Owns-the-Water, said, "You came to us for protection, eh?"

Owns-the-Water ignored the insult. The tall Blue Sleeves was young and obviously knew nothing of Real People. Looking away, his eyes met those of Rabbit-Boss for a moment, and despite their enmity, the two Indians exchanged a knowing glance of amusement. Then Owns-the-Water remembered himself and looked away. Of *course* the miserable Digger knew Mojave were quite capable of defending their own property if they had to. Hadn't they been taught often enough to stay away from certain small irrigated plots of what a stranger might take for open desert?

Across the room, his finger back on the wall map, Lodge was saying, "All right, this fool map Fremont's Expedition drew a few years ago isn't too accurate in the first place, and a lot of it's still blank in the second. We're not going to figure out what Diablito's

51

doing out there to the southwest by jawing about it here at Havasu. How many men do you think you'll need, Lieutenant Caldwell?"

"Sir?"

"Men. How many? Haven't you been listening to a word I've said, goddamn it?"

"Yes, sir, I've been listening, but Captain, I just got here!"

"So what? What do you think they sent you out here to do, peel potatoes? This is the Indian fighting army, Mister, and right now it looks like we have us some Indians who need fighting! I want you to muster a heavy patrol, bead it out, and round those rascals up!"

"On *camels,* sir?"

"Of course on camels. This *is* the Camel Corps, Mister. What's the matter with you? Why are you standing there like a big-ass bird with that stupid look on your face? You surely don't figure to go out after mounted Apache on foot, do you?"

"No, sir, but, damn it, I don't know how! Until this afternoon, I'd seen exactly one camel in my life, and that was in the Philadelphia zoo. High Jolly led me in from the steamboat like a kid on a pony, and my stomach still hasn't gotten over it. I don't know how to manage one camel, let alone a patrol!"

Lodge nodded. "You'll need Greenberg and his tame Digger here, of course. I can't spare more than a dozen camels, so you'd better get Corporal Muller's squad and . . . Yeah, that makes it you two, Muller, and eight troopers. You'll want to take High Jolly along, so it comes out just right."

Greenberg said, "A corporal's squad agin' about a hundred Apache seems to be cuttin' it a mite thin if you ask me, Cap."

Lodge said, "I didn't ask you, Greenberg. Your job is to *find* the Indians. Lieutenant Caldwell and his patrol will do the rest."

He saw the look that passed between the scout and

his new junior officer, and soothed, "We know most of the band consists of women and children. Diablito can't have more than thirty or forty braves with him. Eight-to-one odds are acceptable this side of the Mississippi. Why, when Fremont rode against the hostiles on the other side of the Sierras in the late forties, he was outnumbered fifty to one and . . ."

"Now hold on, damn it!" Greenberg cut in. "That squaw-killer Fremont made his Injun fightin' reputation agin' *Mission* Injuns who never wanted to fight in the first damn place! We ain't talkin' about Mission Injuns now, Cap. If that band out there is Diablito's, we're talkin about *Apache!*"

Lodge shrugged and, turning to Caldwell, asked, "Are you afraid of those odds, Lieutenant? I suppose I could let you have another squad if it's too big for you."

Matt Caldwell shook his head and insisted, "Captain, I'm in no position to lead one squad, two squads, or a blue-tail fly, mounted on camel! I keep trying to tell you, I don't know how to ride the damn things!"

Captain Lodge said, "You'd better start learning, then. You're moving out in the morning. Tell High Jolly I said to pick out a gentle mount for you and, while there's still a little daylight left, have him show you what he can over at the corral."

Caldwell frowned. "Are you serious, sir?"

"Do I look like a man indulging himself in a joke, Mister?"

"No, sir, but, well, I thought Lieutenant Gordon would want to be in command of the patrol, seeing as he's been here at Fort Havasu the longest and . . ."

Lodge's voice cracked like a whip as he cut in with, "You *thought,* Mister? When in thunder did they start asking second lieutenants to think in this man's army?"

Then, Lodge added in a gentler tone, "I know I've given you a hard row to hoe, Mister, but I've got my reasons. I'll expect you to move out at dawn. Is that clear?"

"Yes, sir, but may I ask a couple of questions?"

"No, Mister, you may not. If you aim to learn to ride a camel before the sun goes down, you'd better get cracking!"

THE UNGER PARTY moved at a slow walk into the glowering eye of the setting sun. The dormant scrub of the wide flat they were crossing was turning an orange-dusted purple in the gloaming light, and the view out the arched canvas rear of the prairie schooner might have seemed attractive under other circumstances. Alfrieda sat on the tailgate, bare legs dangling, in the seat vacated by Freddy Dodd. It seemed a mite easier to breathe back there, but the sun was still hot and the girl was too dulled by the long, thirsty afternoon to notice the first star in the lavender eastern sky. Her little brother, Willy, moaned again from where he lay with his head across his mother's cramped thighs.

Alfrieda thought of offering to spell her mother with Willy again, but that would mean moving farther into the stifling interior under the sun-baked canvas top. She knew she was being selfish, and she knew she ought to be ashamed, but maybe if she just kept quiet, Jezebel would offer to hold Willy for a while. Alfrieda knew Momma wouldn't *ask* the Negro maid to do it. Momma seemed embarrassed to have a servant, even though Poppa had bought the girl to help Momma, just before he'd gone out west to open his new store. Maybe, if Jezebel didn't have sense enough to ask, Momma would *order* her to help this once. It wasn't as if Jezebel had any choice, after all. What was it made Momma so bashful about making Jezebel earn her keep? When *she* grew up and had bond servants of her own, there'd be no shilly-shallying around about who did what in *her* house!

Alfrieda half closed her eyes, picturing the house she was going to have someday, when the Right Man came along. The Right Man was still a little blurred in her fourteen-year-old mind, and it was only important that he be tall, handsome, and as nice as Poppa. But the House had been planned in loving detail, from the bright brass knocker on the front door to the rose-and-grape-covered arbor in the back garth. Her Momma had told her once that roses and grape vines were not practical on the same arbor, so Alfrieda had planned the rest of the house in the privacy of her own secret heart, and she was sure, when she met . . . *him,* that roses and grapes would twine together into a perfectly marvelous arbor that everyone in the neighborhood would admire, so there.

Behind her, Alfrieda heard Jezebel murmur, "Let me hold the chile for a spell, Mizz Ernestine. You look purely wore out and that's a fact!"

But Ernestine Unger sighed and said, "It's best not to move him, dear. Besides, there's just no way to get comfortable in this awful wagon, and we'll be stopping soon. The boys said they'd make camp as soon as it started to get dark. Ramon said something about not wanting to move around too much at dusk. Snakes, you know."

Jezebel shuddered. "That Ramon's a snake his own-self if you ask me, Mizz Ernestine. I swear, I still don' see why you up an' hired that uppity Mexican and the trashy white boy he hangs out with!"

Ernestine warned, "Be quiet, they'll hear you!" But Jezebel just shrugged and said, "I don' care does they hear me or doesn't they! Besides, they can't hear what we-all say back here. They too busy up front talkin' to each other about stealin' you blind!"

"Oh, come now, Jezebel, the boys aren't plotting to steal anything from us."

"No, Mizz Ernestine? Then why they always got they heads together like a pair of hogs in the same trough iffen they ain't bad-mouthin' ahint yo' back? How come that Ramon don't drive the team from back here like a natural man? Does you ask me, it's just an excuse to git off by themselves to talk 'bout us!"

"Pshaw! You know the mules have been balky since we left the river, Jezebel! Ramon says mules are likely to bolt in dry country if they smell water ahead, and he's been walking all this way without a word of complaint."

"Without a word of any kind, you mean, Mizz Ernestine. That's a mean-hearted Mexican and that's the truth!"

Ernestine pursed her lips and tried to sound firm. "I don't want to hear any more of these suspicions of yours, Jezebel. I have enough to worry about between Willy's fever and the way our money's running out."

The maid-servant shrugged and looked away, confused as always about the way white folks carried on about their money. As a slave, Jezebel had a hazy knowledge of finances at best. Mizz Ernestine gave her a few coins from time to time, and Jezebel knew the price of such play-pretties as ribbon-bows and paper fans. Once back in Atlanta, Mizz Ernestine had given her some folding money and sent her to the market, but when she'd come back without the right change, Mizz Ernestine had allowed she'd been slickered by them sassy free niggers down to the market, and after that, Mizz Alfrieda had been sent along to oversee her shopping. A couple of times, Mizz Alfrieda had yelled and carried on at the free nigger at the produce stand and said he was a cheat. White folks were a pure caution when it came to counting pennies.

Wrapped in her own silence, Ernestine Unger was aware she shouldn't have voiced concern about money in front of a servant. But she was terribly worried about the way her Hansel's money seemed to be slip-

ping between her fingers along the way. She knew he'd
sent more than enough to see her and the children
across the Great American Desert. Her Hansel was a
shrewd businessman who knew the price of everything,
and he would have sent more if more was required.
Hansel had said, in the letter that accompanied the
bank draft, that he'd made careful inquiries about
prices on the Overland Trail, and allowing for emer-
gencies, he'd sent ten percent more than they could
possibly need.

She'd been foolish, she knew. Most of the money
was gone, despite her best efforts to be a prudent,
dutiful wife, and while she knew her Hansel would
forgive her—Hansel always forgave her womanly
weaknesses—Ernestine Unger was heartily ashamed
of the way she'd managed the trip so far. The young
men she'd hired said the supplies Ramon had bought
for her from that Mexican on the Gila would last them
the rest of the way to Los Angeles City. But there was
the matter of their wages, and unless they made better
time across this last stretch of desert than she had any
right to hope for, she was going to have to make them
wait for the last of their wages. Ramon was already
acting sulky, since the medicinal brandy had given out,
and if he insisted on any more money between here
and the coast, she didn't know how in the world she
was going to cope with the matter.

Out front, leading the team, Ramon and Freddy
Dodd trudged on, eyes and hat brims down as they
walked into the glaring sunset. Freddy was filled with
nervous energy, but Ramon was tired and becoming
insistent on ending the farce. He said, "Every step is
taking us further from water, *amigo*. Why don't we
stop here and be done with it?"

Freddy said, "It's still broad daylight. I thought you
said we'd wait till it started gettin' dark?"

Ramon replied, "The sun is taking forever to set.
Besides, who is there to see what we intend to do?
We are miles from everyone here on this flat. Go back

and get the six-shooter. Tell them we are stopping here."

Freddy pointed with his chin at the western horizon and insisted, "Listen, we oughta wait till we reach them hills up ahead. There'll be water at the base of them hills and . . ."

"Pobrecito!" snorted Ramon, not even looking up from the dust of the trail, "Those hills you see in the distance are a full day's walk from here! You do not wish to wait until we reach the far edge of this flat. You have lost your nerve!"

"That ain't so!" protested Freddy. "I jest want to wait a mite, is all. I jest don't cotton to the notion of shootin' folks in broad daylight out here in front of God and ever'body!"

Ramon pulled the lead mule to a halt. "You don't have to watch. I'm stopping here and sending you to gather greasewood for the campfire, eh?"

"Come on, Ramon. Jest a mite further?"

Ramon didn't answer. Something whirred and thunked, and Freddy stared open-mouthed at the feathered shaft of the arrow that had taken Ramon just over the heart, as the Mexican dropped the lead rein and staggered sideways off the trail. A second and third arrow thunked into Ramon and he fell from sight in the greasewood, and then something hot as fire lanced into Freddy's side and he gasped, "Jesus!" He half turned to run as three more arrows hit him, snuffing consciousness forever from his brain. From somewhere in the sunset's glare, a gruff voice shouted, *"Dikah!"* and the Nadene broke cover.

Inside the wagon, Ernestine and Jezebel exchanged puzzled glances as the shouted command of Kaya-Tenay reached them through the hot canvas. On the tailgate, Alfrieda frowned out at the apparent emptiness of the desert. Then, as if by magic, the startled girl found herself staring at the apparition of a running Indian!

He was naked, save for a deerskin breechclout and

knee-high moccasin-boots. His long black hair was bound with a twisted red bandana, and a white stripe had been painted across his face just below the wide-set, catlike eyes. Those eyes were fixed on Alfrieda as she suddenly came unstuck and tried to pull her legs up into the wagon. The frightened girl moved a split second too late. Eskinya grabbed an ankle in one hand, pulled, and Alfreida Unger found herself sitting on the dusty trail, her thin cotton skirt around her hips, as the Indian jumped over her to catch the edge of the tailgate with his free hand.

His right hand held a twelve-inch blade as he half climbed, half slithered over the tailgate, eyes cold and wary in the gloom. Both women screamed as they cowered from the young Nadene, and Eskinya froze, knife poised, to take the situation in at a glance. Then he pointed at Ernestine with the tip of his blade and asked in awkward Spanish, *"Demelo usted tiswin! Demelo usted,* umm . . . wee-skee?"

Jezebel gasped, *"No tengo* whiskey, *señor!"* and some of the urgency left Eskinya's face as he asked, *"Es verdad?* No wee-skee? No tequila?"

Ernestine asked, "For God's sake, do you understand him, Jezebel?" and the maid-servant said, "A mite, ma'am. My momma was solt from Cuba, an' he's askin' for drinkin' likker in Spanish!"

"Oh, God, we don't have any whiskey left! What are we to do?" Jezebel murmured, "I don' know, ma'am. I reckon they aim to rape us. Maybe, do we pleasure them a lot, they won't scalp us afterwards."

Ernestine Unger swallowed the scream in her throat and hugged her delirious son to her breast. She was afraid to look at the savage, grinning lewdly at her from the rear opening of the wagon. She was trying very hard to wake up.

Out on the trail to the rear, Alfrieda crouched in the dust, her bare feet and naked legs gathered inside the meager protection of her thin cotton skirt. A circle of Indians stood around her, staring down impassively.

Alfrieda pasted a smile across her numb lips and husked, "How?" That was the way you were supposed to say hello to Indians, wasn't it?

None of the Indians answered. Most of them were dressed and painted like the man who'd pulled her from the wagon. A couple had on white Mexican smocks sashed at the waist. All carried spears. Most had short, thick bows either slung over a shoulder or carried loosely in their left hands. Two had rifles. None of the weapons seemed to be pointed at her, and the Indians didn't seem interested in doing anything at all at the moment. They just stood there waiting, and Alfrieda wondered what they were waiting for. Was she supposed to do something? Were they waiting for her to make the first move?

Alfrieda hardly breathed, while the Indians stared. Maybe if she was very still, things might stay that way for a while.

MATT CALDWELL CLENCHED his jaws to keep his teeth from chattering in the pre-dawn desert chill. He'd assembled his patrol before sun-up, wanting to move out at sunrise and aware of the time-consuming details of any military formation. The eight privates of Corporal Muller's squad were dark blurs as they stood lined up for inspection. Across the parade ground, a camel bawled unseen from the corral as High Jolly fed and watered the mounts. The Muslim had said it was important to let them drink their fill in advance. High Jolly had never read the accounts assuring one a camel could last indefinitely without food and drink, and seemed to think they needed to be treated much more like flesh and blood than current remount regulations called for.

Neither Digger Greenberg nor his companion, Rabbit-Boss, had seen fit to fall out for roll call and inspection. The burly quarter-breed, in fact, had threatened the trooper sent to wake him with bodily harm. The two scouts were awake, however, and Matt supposed they'd join the others in their own good time. Both the captain and the other lieutenant, Gordon, were still in bed. It was still an hour before first call.

Corporal Muller had finished his roll call and asked the lieutenant, with a salute, whether he was ready to inspect the men. It seemed an exercise in futility, but Caldwell knew it was expected of him.

Caldwell started down the line, staring at the barely visible faces as if he expected to notice something worth commenting on. The troopers were dragoons, rather than cavalry, so no sabers were in evidence. Each man had been issued two dragoon pistols, a short-barreled musket, and a sword bayonet, along with canteen and cartridge boxes. The muskets and six-shooters were the same .44-caliber, making it possible to use the same paper cartridge and Minie ball in either weapon. This meant a pistol that kicked like a mule and an underpowered musket, but that was the way Jefferson Davis had wanted it, and in truth, there was a certain amount of sense to the idea. Supplies were uncertain on the frontier, and the dragoons, although expected to fight like infantry once they'd ridden to the site of a battle, tended to fire from their mounts and fight the Indians on the run. The bayonets came in handy as oversized daggers on occasion, but the nearly useless saddle muskets simply went along to satisfy someone back in Washington who'd doubtless had a friend or relation in the arms industry.

Caldwell recognized the face of the man who'd led Digger Goldberg's camel from the river boat the previous afternoon, and decided to throw a test question at him. "Soldier, what's your seventh general order?"

The man just stood there, mouth open and a look of utter terror in his pale gray eyes.

Caldwell repeated his question and the trooper stammered, *"Bitte, mein Herr?"*

Corporal Muller cut in with, "Private Dorfler don't speak English, sir. He's a greenhorn from the old country."

Caldwell frowned. "Jesus H. Christ! How many of these men *do* speak English?"

"All but Dorfler savvy most orders, sir. I got two other German boys, two Micks, and a Polack. Rogers and Streeter are Yanks like me."

Caldwell nodded, aware how many immigrants were recruited, almost literally, from the eastern docks. Three-fourths of the enlisted men were foreign-born these days. Most of the recruited immigrants were German or Irish. His fellow officers were divided on which breed made the best soldier. The Irish started with the advantage of speaking English. The Germans, on the other hand, were better about obeying such orders as they understood. Leading a man into a possible battle without his knowing a word of English, however, was a little thick.

Caldwell told Muller, "I want this man replaced with a soldier who speaks English. Go tell the sergeant major I said you were to take a man from Corporal Novak's squad."

Muller hesitated a moment before he stammered, "Permission to disagree, sir?"

"Go ahead, what is it?"

"Private Dorfler's a good soldier and a good *cameleer*, sir. I mean, I talk enough Mohawk Valley Dutch to keep him aimed right and . . ."

"What if something happened to *you*, Corporal Muller? I don't speak a word of German and . . ."

"Begging the lieutenant's pardon, Privates Hess and Von Linden do. If you was to just tell either of them what you wanted old Dorfler to do . . ."

Caldwell laughed. "All right, if you want him that bad, it's your squad, Corporal."

Muller beamed, and Caldwell heard a pleased murmuring among the men before the corporal remembered himself and snapped, "As you were, damn it!"

The squad fell silent, and Caldwell, pleased himself with the way things were going with his new command, said, "At ease, men. I guess the corporal's given you most of it, but we're moving out at sun-up and I figure we'll be on the trail at least seventy-two hours. We've a few minutes of darkness left, so there'll be no excuse for forgetting gear or wanting a piss call less than an hour on the trail. We'll reassemble at the corral in fifteen minutes. Any questions?"

A trooper raised his hand and, when Caldwell nodded at him, said, "The sutler says no man is to leave the post without he settles up his tobacco and notions chit, sir."

Caldwell said, "The sutler's a civilian with no authority over any man here. He can cut off your credit if your bills at his store get too high. He doesn't have anything to say about your comings and goings on or off duty."

There was another pleased murmur, and Caldwell made a mental note to look into the matter if and when he got back. The civilian sutlers who kept shops on military posts under franchise from the War Department were notorious for taking advantage of the underpaid troops. If the one at Havasu was actually giving orders to these immigrant lads, it was time an officer filled him in on a few facts of life.

Another trooper, with an odd accent, asked, "Is true we ride against Apache, *Pan* Lieutenant?"

Caldwell nodded and said, "A band from south of the border reported in the area. What's the problem, uh, Csonka?"

The Polish immigrant shot a sideways glance along the line and opined, "Is few men for fight Apache, *nie?*"

It was a sage assessment, but Caldwell soothed, "We're only moving out a probing action. We don't know this band of Diablito's has jumped the border to fight anybody."

Csonka asked, "If they don't look for fight, *Pan* Lieutenant, why they jumping border in first place?"

"That's a good question. It's one of the things we're riding out to find an answer to."

"*Dlaczego,* I mean why . . . why don't we take full platoon, *Pan* Lieutenant?"

Caldwell was about to explain the advantages of traveling light on an intelligence-gathering mission when Corporal Muller cut in with, "We're movin' out a squad because the lieutenant *says* we're moving out a squad, God damn your eyes! What in thunder do you think you are, Csonka, some kind of officer, for God's sake?"

Csonka nodded. "Was *kapitan* of *straz* one time in old country." Muller snorted, "Well, you're a buck-ass private now!" and the Pole fell silent with a muttered *"Prawda!"*

Caldwell asked, "Any more questions?" and, when there was no reply, told Muller, "Take over, Corporal. I think there's time for a last smoke before we hit the trail. I'll be over at the corral if you need me."

Leaving the men, Caldwell hurried across to the camel corral as the sky grew lighter in the east. After the humiliating two-hour lesson High Jolly had given him the night before, he knew he was going to have to be led like a child again this morning, but at least he'd have a chance to bone up a bit more on the unlikely field equipment Jefferson Davis had stuck them with.

High Jolly was watering a camel at the low trough running along one wall of the adobe corral. Caldwell glanced over the wall and noted the dark forms of kneeling camels lined up neatly at spaced intervals on the hard-packed earth. Matt nodded at the Muslim and asked, "Were they like that all night? I should think they'd go lame hobbled for hours at a time."

High Jolly murmured something to the camel he held by its nose line and explained, "There is no other way to leave El Jamal for the night, Effendi. Though Allah be more merciful, the thrice unruly beasts run off into the darkness unless one leaves a foreleg doubled and tied under them for discipline."

He patted the neck of the animal he was watering. "As you see, Effendi, a man can cope with one animal at a time. Twenty-four of them free to move about would tax the lamp of Aladdin."

"You should have more help. Surely they didn't plan on one drover tending to this many camels, did they?"

"There were many of us in the beginning, Effendi. My fellow Sons of Islam fared little better than the animals once we had arrived. I, as you see, am on my way to becoming an American. Others were unable to take up new ways, and of course, your people have such strange laws about the love of one man for another."

"What do you mean, High Jolly? Our Good Book teaches us that we should love our fellow man."

"Ah, but in moderation, Effendi. I myself have never cared for the flesh of other men, but in my country such matters are neither unheard of nor punished so severely. Back in the east, when we first arrived, some of my countrymen were beaten and threatened most unpleasantly. The officers said that, had they been American soldiers, the punishment would have been twenty years in prison. Truly, this seems a terrible price to pay for a moment of weakness."

"My God, your friends were caught in the act of sodomy?"

"Only one. The other was taking the part of the man. The officer who made so much trouble about it was as weak as they, for as Allah is my witness, he drank himself into a stupor every night and, it is written, drunkenness is a weakness more shameful than theft."

"Yeah, well, the rules are different over here. How much water does a camel *drink,* anyway? That thing's putting away enough for a full team of mules!"

High Jolly said, "El Jamal needs as much water as any animal of his weight, Effendi. Allah has granted him the ability to store it up before a journey. Near regular supplies of water, he drinks little more than an American gallon each day. But it is written on the cucumber leaf we are going out into the chotts. None of these animals will allow itself to be ridden through the gate until it has put away at least ten gallons or more. I have seen a thirsty Jamal consume thirty gallons at one time, though, in truth, this is not good for any creature."

Caldwell leaned his elbows across the adobe wall and, remembering something he'd read someplace, said, "They store the water in that hump up there, right?"

High Jolly suppressed a chuckle. "Forgive me, Effendi, but your people have strange notions about El Jamal. The hump, as you call it, is solid fat. The water is stored partly in one of the extra stomachs Allah granted every beast who chews a cud. Most, in truth, is simply stored in the bloodstream of El Jamal. As he goes, day by day, without a drink, his blood simply thickens. El Jamal can let his flesh dry out more than other animals. He does not sweat, and heat has small effect on him."

"How long can a camel last without water, High Jolly?"

"Nine days, safely, I have known of some who survived a full two weeks without a bite to eat or drop to drink, but I do not recommend such treatment. El Jamal drops dead at unexpected moments. It is Allah's gift to a creature often mistreated by ignorant men."

Caldwell thought a moment and mused, "A horse needs water once a day. A mule can last nearly three. How far apart are the water holes in this area, High Jolly?"

"The truth is written on the wind, Effendi. According to the map in the captain's office, most wells are found near the *jebeli* . . . I mean, ridges that erupt from the flat desert at intervals of thirty to eighty miles. On the flat chotts between the ridges, there is only water in the rainy season and, though Allah be more merciful, those temporary ponds are poisonous."

"All right, let's say drinking water's fifty miles apart, on an average. Let's say an Apache pony can cover twenty to thirty miles a day. That means Diablito's limited in his ability to play Apache hide-and-seek out there. He's got to make a beeline between water holes and pack at least a day's supply in his canteens. You're sure we can keep our mounts going nine days between drinks, High Jolly?"

"Truly, but what of your men, Effendi? A man must have a quart a day in the heat of the desert. Less water will weaken him and, in a just and merciful universe, a bit more would not be too much to ask."

"All right, how heavy a load can a camel carry in addition to its rider?"

"About a hundred and fifty pounds, Effendi. I am assuming, of course, the rider, his weapons, and so forth weigh no more than two hundred."

"Hmm, three hundred pounds for nine days, and water weighs eight pounds a gallon . . . I think we've *got* those Apache sons of bitches, if Rabbit-Boss can cut their trail!"

The Muslim nodded. "This is the last beast to be watered, Effendi, allow me to hobble it and . . ."

"Why do you want to hobble it?" Caldwell cut in. "We're moving out in a few minutes."

High Jolly explained, "It is better that each rider unhobble his own mount, Effendi. El Jamal remembers small favors."

The Muslim pulled the camel's muzzle from the water trough, and as the animal protested with a low burbling moan, Caldwell reached without thinking to pat its head. High Jolly gasped, *"Baleuk, Effendi!"* and

67

slapped at Caldwell's wrist with his free hand. Startled, the officer drew back just as the big green teeth of the camel snapped together in the space his friendly hand had been!

Caldwell gasped, "Good God!" and the Muslim said, "I meant you no insult, Effendi, but this one is a biter!"

"You can say that again! What in the hell made it snap at me that way?"

"Ah, that, too, is written on the wind, Effendi. Perhaps, at some time in the past, a man who resembled you mistreated this one. El Jamal remembers small favors, and small insults as well. Fortunately, this one only tries to bite officers. Sometimes they start biting everyone, and in his infinite mercy, Allah made El Jamal with tasty flesh and very fine leather to be tanned from a biter's hide. *Inshallah,* there is little else one can do with a rogue, though dishonest men have been known to sell a biter to a fool."

High Jolly led the grumpy camel back to the others and forced it to kneel, yanking the nose ring and husking, *"Kh! Kh!* Thrice-accursed offspring of a twelve-thumbed toad!"

Another voice muttered, "Don't them things smell awful?" and Caldwell saw Greenberg had joined them at the corral. Caldwell asked where Rabbit-Boss was, and Greenberg answered, "Over to the latrine, havin' hisself a shampoo."

"Having himself a what?"

"Shampoo. Somethin' wrong with your ears? Diggers set a heap of medicine in havin' clean hair. Rabbit-Boss whups up this lather from yucca root and, ever' chance he gits, washes out his danged old hair like a gal."

"I didn't know Digger Indians were concerned with personal hygiene."

"Well, mebbe that's 'cause you ain't hung around them much. Most Injuns is cleaner than folks give 'em credit fer. I'll allow they don't smell too clean, but that's on account of the fool ways they scrub down

their nekked hides. You see, yucca root don't smell like
regular soap, and aside from rubbin' herbs all over
themselves, Injuns like to sorta *smoke* themselves like
hams. Rabbit-Boss says he stands over an herb fire because it keeps the bugs offen him, but if you ask me,
he thinks it's some dumb sort of perfume. Time an
Injun gits through smokin' his hide in a smudge of juniper, sage, and sech, he winds up smellin' like a goddamn buffalo robe used once too often fer a smoke
signal!"

High Jolly came back, nodded at Greenberg, and
said, "Your mount is ready for your baggage, Jebel
Achdar."

Greenberg said, "I ain't got no baggage. I keep my
gun and possibles handy on my ownself, sonny."

"As you wish, Jebel Achdar."

This time, Greenberg detected the sly look in the
young Muslim's eye and asked, with a frown, "What's
that A-rab thing you keep callin' me, sonny?"

The drover looked innocent and asked, "Is not your
name Greenberg, Yahudi Effendi?"

"Well, what if it is?"

"Corporal Muller tells me this means Green Mountain in the tongue of your forefathers. Jebel Achdar
means Green Mountain in the tongue of mine."

"Is that supposed to be funny, you boy-buggerin'
A-rab son of a bitch?"

"I thought it was amusing. Perhaps, however, it
would be best if I called you Greenberg and you
stopped calling me sonny. I am not your son, after all,
but you are, you must admit, a green mountain."

The bickering was ended unresolved by the sound
of marching feet. Corporal Muller called his eight men
to a halt, saluted Caldwell, and snapped, "At your
command, sir!"

Despite reading the skimpy camel manual prepared
by the War Department from cover to cover the night
before, Matt Caldwell had not the slightest notion how
one ordered a squad of Camel Dragoons to unhobble

and mount their ugly beasts. He returned the corporal's salute gravely and said, "Have your men in the saddle and ready to go in five minutes, Corporal Muller. I just want a last word with the captain before we move out."

He turned to High Jolly and added in a desperately casual voice, "Would you bring my mount over to the orderly room, Mr. Jolly?"

Then, before anyone could ask embarrassing questions, Matt turned and walked away. There was nobody in the orderly room at this hour, and the map, if he'd been able to read it in this light, was inaccurate. It was only a ploy to cover the fact that he was in completely over his head, but hopefully, most of the men would think he knew what he was doing.

Behind him, someone snickered, and Muller snapped, "As you were, damn it!"

Except for Private Dorfler, who didn't know what he was doing there either, none of the men was fooled for a minute, but as one of them observed softly to a companion in the line, "I 'spect he means well and he ain't so bad for a goddamn *officer*."

DAWN FOUND THE band of Kaya-Tenay camped for the day in a dry-wash, for Nadene didn't move their women and children when the sun was shining. The wash was twelve miles west of Fort Havasu, albeit not on the ordnance map in Captain Lodge's office. The Indians, in turn, were unaware of the camel patrol moving south, between their hiding place and the rising sun. After ambushing the Unger party and taking certain precautions to cover their trail, the Nadene had made a night march of nearly thirty miles and were simply resting as they waited for the sun to wend its weary way across the cobalt sky.

Had anyone asked Kaya-Tenay where he was, the husky Nadene would have cheerfully admitted he had no idea. Yet Kaya-Tenay was not lost. Unlike even the most experienced white frontiersman, Kaya-Tenay carried a rough map of the western third of the continent in his bones. He knew, without thinking about it, that most of the mountain ranges and their intervening valleys ran northwest to southeast no matter where one traveled in what the map-makers were one day to call the Basin and Range Province. He knew from experience where chaparral gave way to piñon and juniper on any new but hardly unfamiliar ridge. Kaya-Tenay had no word for geology, but he needed no book to tell him that flint for an arrowhead could be found embedded in a chalk escarpment, and that water hid in the alluvial fans of canyons running down from sandstone hills. The minor details of the vast wastelands he and his people roamed were merely small surprises that added spice to days on the everlasting trail. Kaya-Tenay felt at home anywhere between the Humboldt in Nevada Territory to the winding Rio Yaqui of Sonora. Neither Kaya-Tenay nor any member of his band had ever been this far north before, but it hardly mattered. The lay of the land was the same on both sides of the border for mile after endless mile.

The enemy up here wore different clothes and spoke a different tongue, but the same tricks seemed to work no matter where one traveled, and the White Eyes leading the wagon team had been as unaware as others of the possible dangers hidden in a sunset's glare. It was said the snow fell lower on the mountains up here in the northern deserts, but the Moon of the Wolf Winds lay far in the future, and he was certain to have another vision by then. There had been no tiswin in the wagon last night, but there would be other wagons and, with tiswin, or the fiery brown tequila of the White Eyes, all things were possible.

A few yards up the wash, huddled with her children and serving-maid against the steep marl bank, Ernestine Unger watched the morning activity around them, as well as she could with apparently downcast eyes. Where had she ever gotten the idea that the coldest possible stare was that of a gray-eyed Prussian officer? These terrible Indians had eyes of frozen ink. Fortunately, if one held still and neither spoke nor appeared to notice them, the Apache tended to ignore one. Perhaps they were like reptiles, attracted only by movement. Aside from the one who'd spoken Spanish to Jezebel, none of their captors had seemed at all interested in communicating since they'd been hauled, numb with terror, from their wagon.

The long night ride was still a kaleidoscopic blur in Ernestine Unger's fatigue-drugged mind. She had put up a weak struggle when Willy was snatched from her by an Indian on a spotted pony, and was relieved when she saw, from the back of the burro she and Jezebel had been forced to share, that the Indian carrying Willy in one brawny, naked arm seemed gruffly gentle with the sick child.

They'd given Willy back to her, once dismounted in this brushy, sandy gully, and Alfrieda had run over to join them, tear-streaked and tangle-haired, but otherwise seemingly unharmed. Ernestine had no idea what had happened to the two young men out in front with the team. She'd hoped they'd got away, but one of those mules just down the gully with the Indian ponies looked a lot like one from her own team.

Her thoughts were abruptly interrupted when a dark, pockmarked boy of ten or twelve came over to them with a basket, knelt to place it on the sand near Jezebel, and murmured, *"Que lo aproveche, señora."*

Jezebel quickly asked, *"Habla 'Spañol?"* and the boy smiled shyly and said, *"Si, señora, soy de Sonora en Mejeco."*

"You a Mexican?" Jezebel asked in Spanish. The boy looked uncertain and answered in the same language, "I used to be Mexican. Now, I think, I am Nadene. My new father's name is Kaya-Tenay. He says I am not to speak of my old family. It is bad medicine to speak the names of the dead."

Ernestine nudged her maid-servant and asked what she and the boy were talking about. Jezebel explained, "He's brung us a basket of vittels, ma'am. He says he's a Mexican boy these Apaches run off with, like ussen."

The boy caught the word "Apache" and cautioned Jezebel in Spanish, "It is best to call my people Nadene, señora. Apache means 'enemy' in the tongue of the Pueblos. You and your friends are in no position to remind them they are not your friends, *comprendas?*"

A middle-aged woman up the dry-wash shouted, "Digoon!" and the Mexican boy murmured, "I must go. Cho-Ko-Ley said I was to gather water for the ponies after feeding you."

He stood up and moved away as Jezebel frowned, trying to understand that business about . . . *gathering* water? Her Spanish was probably rusty.

Meanwhile, Ernestine had removed the lid from the basket and was examining its contents dubiously. She had no way of knowing her captors were on short rations, and neither the parched corn nor the jerked venison looked very appetizing. She reached in uncertainly and handed a sliver of jerky to Alfrieda. As Esnestine gave another piece to Jezebel, Alfrieda took an experimental taste and said, "Pooh, it's as hard and dry as an old chair rung!"

Something thudded to the sand nearby, and they looked up to see the woman who'd called the Mexican boy away. She was wearing a shapeless cotton smock and knee-high moccasin-boots. Her moonface, framed by wings of gray-streaked hair, was totally devoid of expression. As Jezebel reached for the Mexican army canteen that Cho-Ko-Ley had dropped to them, the Nadene woman stared blankly down at the feverish boy, whose head was held in Ernestine's lap once more.

73

Cho-Ko-Ley searched her memory for the few words of Spanish she knew. Then she asked, not looking at anyone in particular, *"Que pasa? Es enfermo?"*

Jezebel nodded and in Spanish said, "The boy has a fever. He has been sick since we crossed the Colorado. Do you have any quinine?"

Cho-Ko-Ley said, "No," and turned to walk away without another word. Jezebel shrugged and said, "At least she gave us water. You want me to tear a rag offen my shimmy skirt and wet it for Master Willy, ma'am?"

The worried mother nodded as Alfrieda, forcing down a bit of jerky, opined, "Mean old Apache squaw don't care does Willy die or get well. You see the way she looked at him, Momma? She looked pure daggers through poor Willy, that's what she did."

Jezebel tore a patch from the hem of her petticoat and reached for the canteen as she explained, "I asked did they have medicine, but she said they didn't, ma'am. Maybe a damp rag on his forehead will help him break the fever and . . ."

"It's no use!" Ernestine sobbed, rocking the dying child's head in her lap as she bent over him, as if to shield him from the Angel of Death with her breast. Willy's flesh was hot and dry, and he'd stopped moaning or trying to move in her arms. He was dying. She knew he was dying. The prayers she'd said were as meaningless as a mother's tears in this godless, endless wasteland. What was it that Freddy Dodd had said about no law west of the Pecos, and no God west of Apache Pass? She'd laughed the first time she'd heard it. How was she to have known it was no joke?

Jezebel held the damp rag out until she saw her mistress was ignoring it. Then she touched Ernestine gently on one arm. "Let me take him for a mite, ma'am. You're plumb wore out and you oughta eat some."

Alfrieda looked up, saw her mother's dazed expression, and moved closer, saying, "Let Jezzie take him,

Momma. You ain't helpin' him, holdin' him like that."

"She ain't listenin', Mizz Frieda," said the servant-maid. "She's off someplace where she can't hear."

Alfrieda nodded, but put two firm hands on her mother's shoulders and said, "Take Willy away from her and sponge his head, Jezzie."

"She don't look like she aims to let him go, Mizz Frieda."

"You do as I say, Jezzie. Momma ain't herself and we have to do right by my little brother."

The slave girl hesitated and Alfrieda insisted, "You do like I say, hear?"

"Mizz Frieda, you ain't but fourteen years old, and . . ."

"I'm old enough to see my momma can't think straight, you sassy nigra! You just tend to Willy and let me worry about how old I am!"

Jezebel shrugged, reached out for the sick child and, as Alfrieda held her bewildered mother, moved Willy to a more comfortable position with his head down and covered with the damp cloth. Ernestine struggled mindlessly for a moment, whimpered, and suddenly buried her head against Alfrieda's breast. The adolescent held the frightened woman in her thin, strong arms and soothed, "It's all right, Momma. Everything's going to be all right. I won't let them hurt you or Willy."

MATT CALDWELL WAITED until high noon before he made his big mistake. They'd ridden nearly twenty miles southwest of Fort Havasu at the mile-eating, maddening gait of a walking camel, when Caldwell called a break.

The midday break was not the mistake. The men were stiff and tired after more than six hours in the uncomfortable Tuareg saddles, and the overhead sun was becoming a hellish open furnace door in the sky.

Greenberg's Indian tracker, Rabbit-Boss, had walked all the way ahead of the column and took immediate advantage of the break to crawl under a mesquite and take a nap. The others made their camels kneel and climbed stiffly off, cursing, relieving themselves in the bushes, and searching for slivers of partial shade to eat their dry rations in a bit of comfort.

The mistake Matt Caldwell made was when, near the end of the twenty-minute break, he decided it was time he tried to control his camel on his own. High Jolly had held the lead for him since leaving the fort, and he was sure his mount by now had gotten used to the idea that he was in command of this patrol. It was all very well for Greenberg to be led about by Trooper Dorfler. The scout was only on temporary duty with the Camel Corps and made no bones about his dislike for the ungainly animals. To Greenberg, the camel was only a means to get across the desert without walking. When it came to the serious business of fighting Indians, Greenberg preferred to stand on his own two feet.

But Caldwell felt ridiculous leading a patrol on a mount he couldn't control. Before ordering his men to mount up again, he decided to put the matter to rights. The twelve camels were kneeling in a hobbled line, apparently oblivious to their hot and dry surroundings as they belched and burbled, chewing their cuds. Fatima, the mare camel High Jolly had selected for the lieutenant, had been hobbled near a clump of American saltbush that was close enough to camel's-thorn to serve as fodder. As Caldwell approached, Fatima's snakelike neck stretched out for another mouthful of saltbush, and when he said, "We're going for a little ride, Fatima," his soothing words evoked a look of bland disinterest from under the camel's heavy eyelids.

Taking the rein in one hand, Caldwell leaned to loosen the slip-knot noose that kept Fatima's left foreleg doubled under her. In the middle distance, High Jolly called, "No, Effendi!" as the officer climbed up into Fatima's saddle and shouted, *"Arrah, arrah,* get up, old girl."

Fatima twisted her serpentine neck to stare back at him in utter contempt, as Caldwell repeated the command he'd heard High Jolly and the others give to make their camels rise. High Jolly was running over, yelling something in Arabic, as Fatima belched, groaned, and suddenly lurched to her feet. Pleased with himself, Caldwell kicked his heels against the flat dun sides of the big animal and muttered, *"Hike! Hike!* Giddy-*up,* goddamn it!"

For a moment, nothing seemed to happen. Then Fatima lurched forward and started in the general direction of the Atlantic Ocean at a dead run!

A camel walks a little slower than a marching soldier. It runs much faster than a horse. There are no stages in between. Full speed is a series of stilt-legged jolts, and Caldwell was immediately sorry he'd started the whole thing. Clinging to the high cruciform pommel with one hand, he hauled back on the rein as hard as he could with the other and gasped, "Whoa! Shhh! Shhh!" and when that didn't work, he tried to turn the brute at least by yelling, *"Adda! Adda!* Where in the hell do you think you're going, you lop-eared crazy bitch?"

Fatima neither swerved nor slowed as she bounced east on her long, stiff-kneed legs. The saddle bobbed from side to side on the flabby hump, and Caldwell was having enough trouble staying aboard *before* the right stirrup strap gave way. He clung desperately for a few more strides, half out of the saddle at a crazy forty-five-degree angle, and then he muttered, "The hell with it," and concentrated on holding the end of the rein as he fell.

The desert came up to meet him with a bone-jarring thump, and then he was dragging through the dust and gravel on the end of the braided leather line, cursing and spitting dirt and smashed greasewood brush from between split lips as the camel fought the drag of his dead weight.

And then Fatima gave up, as suddenly as she'd begun, and dropped her bleeding nose to nibble disdainfully at a creosote bush. Matt Caldwell watched narrowly, lying on his elbows and clinging to the line for all he was worth. But the camel had apparently decided she'd had enough.

High Jolly ran past, grabbed the rein near the nose ring, and smashed a camel goad across Fatima's head, shouting, *"Kh! Kh!* On your knees, Daughter of Ahriman!"* as he forced the runaway to kneel. As Caldwell got weakly to his feet, High Jolly looked back and said, "You did well to hold on to the rein, Father of Meharim! If you had let go, this thrice-accursed beast would not have stopped this side of the Colorado!"

"Yeah, well, give me that goad and wait here until I find the damn stirrup I threw back there. I think I'm getting the hang of it."

"Effendi, you cannot be serious! We are not in the corral back at the fort. If she throws you again out here in the open, there will be no catching her. None of the others can run as fast with a man in the saddle as Fatima can without!"

"She might throw me, High Jolly, but she's not going to make me let go unless she kills me first."

As Caldwell turned away, High Jolly sighed, "I fear Fatima knows this, too, Effendi."

Looking back the way he'd come, Matt Caldwell was surprised at the distance. The rest of his patrol seemed far away, except for Corporal Muller, who'd followed High Jolly and was now approaching with the lost stirrup in one hand. From where he stood, holding Fatima's bridle, the Muslim called, "Talk to the Effendi Lieutenant, friend Muller! He is determined to master this stubborn mother of stampedes!"

Muller came over to give Caldwell the stirrup, saying, "If the lieutenant won't mind a suggestion, me and High Jolly could maybe ride on either side and . . ."

"Just let me buckle that son-of-a-bitch stirrup right and stand clear, Corporal," Caldwell cut in, limping over to Fatima to replace the loosened strap. Standing near the camel's head, High Jolly insisted, "Listen, Effendi, you will lose this mount, even if you don't break your neck! I told you back at the fort it takes at least a week to learn the art of the Mehari!"

Muller added, "She smells the river, Lieutenant. The wind's from the east and these critters go loco when they taste water in the air."

Caldwell insisted, "She's not thirsty. She's just ornery. But you know how the old song goes, there was never a critter that couldn't be rode?"

"Yes, sir, and never a rider that couldn't be throwed! Do you lose your mount, sir, we're gonna have to double two men up on one of the camels."

But Caldwell was climbing up into the saddle with a firm expression. He asked, "Have either of you seen my hat?" and Muller answered, "Yes, sir, it's in that clump of pear yonder." Caldwell nodded and said, "Pick it up for me and hang on to it, will you?" Then he turned to High Jolly and said, "Give me that rein and untie the hobble, drover."

"Effendi, do you think this is wise?"

"No, but turn her loose and let her buck!"

The Muslim shrugged, muttered, "Inshallah, he will live through this fall as well as he did the last," and did as he was told.

For a moment, nothing happened. Then Caldwell kicked and shouted, *Arrah! Arrah!* Let's see you do that again, you oversized cross between a rocking chair and a nanny goat!"

Slowly, Fatima got to her feet, moaned, and turned her head toward the east. Caldwell pulled the rein, slammed her on the side of the head with the camel goad, and insisted, *"Adda! Adda!* Turn around or I'll break your goddamn skull!"

Fatima burbled, groaned, and majestically turned, as if that was what she'd had in mind all the time. Caldwell saw Muller had his hat and swung the camel toward the corporal, saying, *"Hot-hot-hot!"* to slow Fatima's pace as he leaned over and grabbed his hat on the fly with a desperately nonchalant nod of thanks. He replaced the dusty hat on his disheveled hair and walked the camel back toward the others. A cheer went up from the dismounted cameleers and Caldwell shot them a stern look. What was the matter with the idiots? Hadn't they ever seen a man ride a camel before?

BY THREE P.M. the temperature had stabilized at a hundred and twenty-six degrees in the shade, and there was, of course, no shade atop a moving camel. The movement helped, creating the effect of a three-knot breeze as the column plodded southwest. The instant evaporation of sweat in the bone-dry desert air was a mixed blessing. It kept a man from dying of heat prostration, but the crust of salt it left in crotch and armpits of one's uniform itched like hundreds of crawling ants. Matt Caldwell stared dully at the plodding form of Rabbit-Boss, on foot ahead of the column, and envied the Indian his naked state. Under a white man's roof, the "savage" Digger had seemed ignorant and primitive, even by Indian standards. Out here on the trail, his life style was beginning to make a lot of sense. As Greenberg had observed, Rabbit-Boss hadn't refused to wear so much as a breechclout because he was "proud of his pecker," but, simply because anything you put next to your skin in this country itched!

Having more or less mastered his mount, Caldwell had taken the point, although High Jolly kept his own mount within discreet distance for a sudden swoop to the rescue. The Muslim knew, better than Caldwell, how often a camel might simply be waiting for a chance to take advantage of an unsure rider.

On the other side, unwilling to waste his time on foolish notions, Digger Greenberg rode his own mount, led by Trooper Dorfler. This freed Greenberg's hands to grip the buffalo rifle across his knees, and if there was occasion to request a change in course, Dorfler understood Greenberg's garbled, half-forgotten Yiddish better than he did the English commands of the lieutenant. Both Greenberg and his Hessian attendant, in fact, thought that what Greenberg referred to as "old country" was some form of German. The scout spoke a bit of Cree from the other side of his family tree, and in time, his twentieth-century descendants would remember him proudly as one of those tall, blond Nordic "mountain men" who'd "tamed the West."

Trooper Dorfler, in turn, was fated to found a petty dynasty of Regular Army noncoms who, once they'd anglicized the name to Dorman, would teach a future Kaiser a good lesson.

Corporal Muller and his squad followed in a line less military than the A.R.'s prescribed. The lieutenant, remembering that the first thing he'd seen of the formation the day before had been the fluttering red and white guidon, had left Muller's squad pennant behind at the fort. It was easy enough to dress a line of twelve camels at close range, and he saw no reason to make it any easier to see at a distance than he had to.

From their high seats on the Turkish saddles, the members of the patrol had well over a five-mile view to the horizon. There didn't seem to be much more than desert pavement and knee-high scrub out there to see. From time to time, a locust whirred out from under a camel's foot, but otherwise the flat they were crossing seemed devoid of animal life. It hardly seemed possible for a lizard to live out here on these flats, let alone a band of Apache.

A hundred yards out front, Rabbit-Boss was aware of all the little eyes that watched him from the surrounding brush. This was partly because he was much closer to the earth than the mounted white men, and partly because he knew the way his universe worked much better than even Greenberg, although, in truth, the big bearded man who'd saved him from the Great Sleep many moons before saw much the others did not. Greenberg was not as foolish as his White-Eyed brothers, who died like untended babes if left alone in the bountiful lands between the mountains.

Rabbit-Boss caught a whiff of what a white man might have smelled as vinegar, and slowed to approach a clump of saltbush dead ahead with caution. He probed the saltbush with his digging stick and murmured, "Go and hide yourself somewhere else, little brother. The Spirit Horses stick their great split noses into this sort of greenery, and your sting would earn you nothing but the Great Sleep!"

The scorpion he'd disturbed scuttled across the gray gravel to the shade of a clump of cholla as in the distance Greenberg called, "What is it, Rabbit-Boss? You spot Apache sign out there, Old Son?"

The Indian tracker moved on without answering. He didn't like to be called Rabbit-Boss, although he understood enough English to understand why the White Eyes laughed at his true name, Wee-Tshitz. Old Son was a stupid name, too. Wee-Tshitz had not been adopted into the maternal clan of Greenberg or any other White Eyes. Under his breath, the Indian repeated "I am Wee-Tshitz, son of Our-Ye-Voka, and Rabbit-Boss of the Sage-Grouse People . . ." and then his eyes began to mist and he swallowed the lump that suddenly grew in his throat. For the Sage-Grouse People were no more. Driven from their old hunting grounds by mounted Bannock, they'd been ambushed and ridden down by raiding Snakes of the Southern Utes. All were caught but him, and only the skill of the White-Eyed Greenberg had saved Wee-Tshitz when the last of the Sage-Grouse People had staggered delirious into that trapper's camp in Arroyo Seco. Heya! That had been a bad Rabbit Moon. Someday he would pay the Southern Utes back for what they'd done. Meanwhile, Greenberg wanted him to find those other mounted Snakes, the ones they called Apache. The Apache had not killed his friends and family, but they rode horses, and to Wee-Tshitz of the Sage-Grouse People all mounted Indians were the same. All deserved a long, bad death before they took the Great Sleep.

Matt Caldwell had dropped back beside Digger Greenberg to ask the scout what the Indian had seen. Greenberg said, "Beats the shit out of me, Lieutenant. Rabbit-Boss reads sign in running water on a dark night."

"He didn't answer when you shouted to him. Is he sulking about something?"

"Don't think so. Injuns ain't polite like you an' me. When your average Injun don't have nothin' to say, he usually keeps his mouth shut. It ain't a thing to git spooked about. When an Injun's really pissed off at you, he lets you know it, same as anyone else. I mind one time on the Milk River a mess of us old boys got some Blackfeet riled at us. I mean, you never heard so much cussin' and singin' and dancin' and carryin' on in your life! I reckon Rabbit-Boss just stopped to have a look-see at a bird turd or somethin'. Injuns take a lot more interest in things than ussen."

Caldwell noticed Rabbit-Boss had slowed again and was bearing a bit to the right. He told Greenberg, "He's turning more to the west. Ask him what the Devil's going on!"

Greenberg spit a jet of tobacco juice on the polite side of his camel. "Don't have to ask. Don't you see them buzzards 'bout a mile off to west-sou'west?"

Caldwell screened his eyes against the afternoon glare and made out a dozen rising motes of black. He said, "I see them going *up!*"

"So?"

"So wouldn't they be going down if something was lying dead over there?"

Greenberg nodded. "They would iffen it was up to them, Lieutenant. The way Rabbit-Boss and me reads it, them buzzards was feedin' yonder, till somethin' spooked them."

Caldwell raised his free hand to halt the column and reached for the dragoon pistol on his hip. Greenberg snorted, "Shoot, it's likely only a coyote, Lieutenant."

"What if you're wrong? What if those buzzards were flushed by *Apache?*"

Greenberg shook his head and said, "Apache don't flush buzzards or nothin' else, Lieutenant. Besides, if Rabbit-Boss thought there was Hoss Injuns up ahead, he wouldn't be joggin' over to see what them buzzards was feedin' on, would he?"

"Doesn't Rabbit-Boss ever make a mistake?"

"About Hoss Injuns? He did once. That's how I come by him in the first place. He come limpin' in outten the Great Basin with a Ute arrow in him couple of seasons back. Like to drank ever' drop of Taos Lightnin' I had in my pack, afore we got him patched up enough to walk agin. The best way I ever put it together, he was off makin' medicine fer a rabbit drive when the Utes hit his folks. They was scalp huntin' fer the Mexicans, and Rabbit-Boss was the onliest one in his band as got away."

Caldwell frowned and asked, "These Horse Utes

were hunting Diggers for the Mexican government on this side of the border?"

Greenberg shook his head. "It was Mexican territory all the way to the Humboldt afore we'uns took it away from 'em in forty-eight. The Utes was gittin' paid, of course, fer *Apache* scalps. But one Injun's scalp looks pretty much like any other's, and besides, them Apache fight back a lot, so . . ."

"I see what you mean. What do the Mexicans pay for a scalp?"

" 'Bout forty Yankee dollars last I heard. The scalp-huntin' trade ain't as good as it used to was, when Scalpin' Jamie Johnson and his gang was gittin' rich at it. Used to be they paid a hundred fer a warrior's scalp, fifty fer a squaw's and twenty-five fer a kid's. But of course, the scalp hunters never turnt in no scalps they allowed was women an children's. Fool Mexicans paid out a heap of warrior bounties on the skinned haids of Pueblo women, and even Mexican gals, afore they wised up."

Greenberg spit again and added, "Governor of Chihuahua won't give dime fer a scalp these days, but Sonora still pays forty and ain't too particular 'bout who it comes from."

"That's crazy! Forty dollars is a fortune to many a white man out here! What good does it do Sonora to pay for the killing of friendly Indians on our side of the border?"

"Don't do them much good at all, Lieutenant. That's likely why the folks in Chihuahua stopped doin' it. But Sonora's populated thin, and the ranchers down thataway are plumb spooked by almost any Injun, so . . ."

"So we're left to fight the hornets' nest these murdering red and white scalp hunters stir up! By God, if I ever get my hands on anyone like this Johnson you were telling me about . . ."

"Ain't no need to get riled," Greenberg cut in. "The scalp trade's goin' the way the beaver trade went. Ain't hardly a white man left in the business, and as fer the Horse Utes, they jest kill Diggers fer practice, whether they's paid or not."

By this time, they were nearing the place where the buzzards had been feeding, and Rabbit-Boss had stopped. Greenberg's camel suddenly pulled back on its lead, and the surprised Dorfler cursed and yanked on the braided line as Caldwell's mount, in turn, began to dance nervously from side to side. Greenberg yelled, *"Schweigst du, Schmo!* The sons of bitches smell dead meat! We'd best go in afoot!"

Caldwell nodded, halted the others with a raised hand, and made the guttural *"Khhh!"* that High Jolly and the others used to make a camel kneel. Fatima danced in a little circle as she considered the suggestion. Then, as High Jólly moved in on one side and Matt Caldwell slammed her head from the other, Fatima sank to her knees with a gargle of complaint. Caldwell rolled off her hump and jogged over to where Rabbit-Boss was standing, looking down at something. At first, Caldwell thought it was a pile of butcher's rags thrown out with meat scraps and a few unsold soup bones. Then the mishapen mass resolved itself into a mangled human form, and Caldwell gagged. Rabbit-Boss said, "Not dead long. Coyotes bury head someplace, I think."

"Do you think it was a white man, Rabbit-Boss?"

"White man, maybe white woman wearing pants and checkered shirt. Buzzards take guts and private parts. That leg bone long for woman. I think this was man, before somebody kill him."

Digger Greenberg had joined them by the time Caldwell asked the Indian, "How do you know he was killed? Couldn't he have died of thirst?"

Rabbit-Boss looked away, disgusted.

Greenberg said, "That's easy, Lieutenant. There ain't no boots."

"I beg your pardon?"

"No boots. What's the matter, you got wax in your ears, Lieutenant?"

"I can see this body's not wearing boots, dammit. As far as that goes, it's not wearing feet!"

"Aw, that's a foot bone over there by that grease-wood clump. But that's not the point. Rabbit-Boss knows he was kilt because somebody took his boots offen him. I mean, neither coyotes nor buzzards has all that much use fer a pair of boots when there's fresh red meat to be had."

"You don't have to draw me a picture."

"Well, keep your damn eyes open, then. What does the sign say, Rabbit-Boss? Which way was this hombre headed when they jumped him?"

Rabbit-Boss shook his head. "Not killed here. Snakes play old trick. Drop dead man here to draw buzzards away from true start of trail."

Greenberg bent to pick a broken twig from the gravel as he mused, "Yeah, I see where they dragged a mess of chamiso brush ahint them to brush out their tracks. I make it two men on foot, packin' this deader betwixt 'em. How do you read it, Old Son?"

The Indian said, "One man, one squaw. Man hold shoulders. Squaw carry feet and drag brush. They drop this here. Go back same way to where others hold ponies."

Matt Caldwell stared down at what to him was absolutely unbroken desert pavement. The winds of centuries had blown away all fine-grained soil, leaving only this hard-packed gray-white gravel. A white man's heel or the hoof of any animal left a noticeable impression in the desert pavement. How Greenberg and his Indian companion could trace the outline of a moccasin track, male or female, was beyond him. He asked the scout, "How far do you think they would have carried the body from where they killed this man?" and Greenberg opined, "Couple of miles mebbe. Depands on what kinda Injuns we're a-dealin' with. What do you say, Rabbit-Boss? You think this old boy was hit by Diggers or Snakes?"

"Snakes," said Rabbit-Boss, not bothering to explain his reasons. If the White Eyes could not see the heel impressions of a man used to spending most of his time on horseback, they were even blinder than he'd thought.

Greenberg spit and said, "Too far south fer Bannock, and Mojave wouldn't have sent that hombre Owns-the-Water in fer a powwow iffen they'd been killin' white folks. So I suspicion we've located Diablito and his band. We'd best circle up and wait fer nightfall afore we head back to the fort."

Caldwell frowned and asked, "What do you mean, head back to the fort? We don't know where Diablito is or which way he's heading!"

Greenberg nodded. "That's a good way to keep it, Lieutenant. Iffen we don't know where he is, them Apache don't know where *we'uns* is."

"Damn it, man, I didn't ride all this way just to turn back at the first Indian sign!"

"You didn't? What in tarnation *did* you have in mind, Lieutenant?"

"Well, I thought our mission was to locate Diablito, find out what he was doing on our side of the border, and . . ."

"That's jest what you done!" Greenberg cut in. "You know he's around here someplace, and you know he's killin' white folks hereabouts. So why don't we shoot back to Fort Havasu, and tell the goddamn captain about it?"

"Come on, you're not afraid of a handful of border-jumping renegades, are you?"

"When they's at least three dozen Nedni-Apache? You just bet your ass I am! Your job out here ain't to *fight* Diablito, Lieutenant. It's to *find* the ornery rascal so's Captain Lodge can chase him home with at least a full troop of dragoons and a couple of field pieces!"

Caldwell had to think about that. His orders had

been vague, and it wasn't clear whether the post commander wanted him to gather intelligence or simply take a dozen camels out and lose them. He knew his Abolitionist `superior had mixed feelings about the Camel Corps. Matt himself was not too keen on making their brilliant, treacherous Secretary of War look good in President Buchanan's fuzzy vision. The weak, well-meaning administration in Washington swung like a weathercock in every political wind, and Jefferson Davis was the biggest wind from the South. If some of his more fantastic schemes were to fail . . .

"We need more information to go on," said Caldwell, his mind made up for the moment. He was a soldier, not a politician, and his mission was to find out what Diablito was doing and, if it was hostile to the United States, put a stop to it.

Digger Greenberg said, "We know all we need to, Lieutenant. Them Apache is hereabouts, and they's on the warpath. What else do you aim to carry back to the captain?"

"The identity of this man, and the name of the tribe that killed him, for openers."

"Shoot, his mother'd never recognize him now, and, as fer who done him in . . ."

"You don't know shit," snapped Caldwell. "The missing boots may or may not indicate he was murdered. He may or may not have been murdered by Indians. As for the tribe we're talking about, you're just guessing and you know it."

"Well, shoot, we know Diablito's jumped the border and . . ."

"We know no such thing, Digger. A Mojave *told* us Apache were over here on this side of the river. Have any of us *seen* one Apache since we left the fort this morning?"

Greenberg spit again. "If you knowed enough to pour piss outten your boots, you'd know better than to expect to *see* Apache." He pointed at the mangled remains at his feet. "Who else would have kilt this old boy here?"

Caldwell threw back, "How the hell should I know? Why couldn't it have been Mojave, or more likely, another white man?"

Greenberg asked Rabbit-Boss, "What do you think, Old Son? You reckon this jasper was kilt by his own people fer his boots?"

The Indian stared soberly at Matt Caldwell for a time before he answered. The Blue Sleeves, he'd decided, was not the fool he'd first appeared. He was wrong, of course: Nadene moccasin prints were not hard to read. But for a White Eyes, the lieutenant was a man who chewed his thoughts before he swallowed them. This was a habit to be encouraged. Too many Real People had been blamed for bad things by White Eyes who acted before they'd taken time to think.

Rabbit-Boss said, "I think we will know better after we trace sign back to where this one was ambushed. Not enough sign here to say what happened.

Digger Greenberg frowned. "goddamn it, Rabbit-Boss, if that ain't an Apache heel mark right there by that quartz pebble, I'll kiss your Injun ass!"

Rabbit-Boss shrugged. "Maybe Apache. Maybe White Eyes in Apache moccasin. Maybe Mojave make big fool of Greenberg. Maybe if we look more, we find out."

Greenberg turned to Caldwell with an apologetic smile. "I can't do nothin' with him when he's got an idear stuck crosswise in his Injun haid, Lieutenant. Old Rabbit-Boss just won't let go that bone until he's chawed it some."

"You just let him chaw, Digger. I'm a curious cuss myself."

"Well, we'd best form a circle and set a spell then. No tellin' how long it's gonna take old Rabbit-Boss to follow the sign back to where . . ."

"This way!" Rabbit-Boss cut in, pointing due west toward a distant ridge of lavender hills. The Indian started jogging across the flat without looking back, and Caldwell asked Greenberg, "You were saying . . . ?"

"Aw, shut up and saddle up. How do you expect me to know what that fool Injun's fixin' to do, when he don't know his ownself?"

THE NADENE PEOPLE did not build fires in strange country during daylight hours, if they could help it. Few white men realized how easy it was to hide the glow of a fire in a depression at night, while far too many learned to their sorrow that rising smoke can be seen for miles in sunlight.

Hence, Kaya-Tenay was as puzzled as he was annoyed when he found his principal wife, Cho-Ko-Ley, setting fire to a small pile of cheat grass against the north wall of the dry-wash. Kaya-Tenay stared soberly up at the western sky and observed, "The sun has not even started to bleed upon the ridges, old woman. I know cheat grass burns with little smoke, but do we have to have smoke at all in broad daylight?"

Cho-Ko-Key said, "I need the fire to brew a Black Drink. There is sickness among us and the fever demons must be taught a lesson."

"The herbs you carry in your medicine bundle are powerful, wisest of my wives, but who is sick? I have just been up and down this arroyo and everyone seems ready to ride this night."

Cho-Ko-Ley shook her head. "The little boy you carried with the other White Eyes from their wagon is half dead from those water demons the Mexicans brought to our rivers. If I can drive them out with Black Drink, the boy may live."

Kaya-Tenay frowned. "You are risking an enemy seeing our smoke for a foolish reason, old woman."

Cho-Ko-Ley nodded. "You should have killed all of the White Eyes in the first place, before I had to listen to the little boy cry."

"I will go over there and kill him for you now. That way, you will not hear him crying and our enemies will not see our smoke."

"You waited too long to make the offer, Kaya-Tenay. I will be careful with my little fire."

"Women!" muttered Kaya-Tenay, walking away without giving or refusing his wife permission to brew her medicinal tea. That was the trouble with taking prisoners. You never knew what to do with them after you had them. Kaya-Tenay wandered down the wash to where young Eskinya was rubbing down a pony with sand. Kaya-Tenay stared at the younger Husband for a time. Then he said, "You should have killed those women when we killed their men. The old one with the yellow hair has a sick child and my principal wife is upset about it."

Eskinya rubbed some more sand on the pony's hind leg and said, "I don't like the looks of this brush cut. I think the flies have been at it and I can't get it to dry up."

"I think somebody ought to kill that yellow-haired woman and her sick child," Kaya-Tenay insisted. "You can have the young virgin and the pretty black White Eyes if you want."

Eskinya rubbed more sand on the pony's sore and straightened up, not looking at the older man as he said, "If my father wishes to fight the little boy, I will have to speak against it as a bad thing."

Kaya-Tenay struggled to keep from losing his temper as he insisted, "*I* don't want to do it! But how far can we carry them, unless they stop crying and start to act like people?"

"The black White-Eyed girl speaks Spanish, my father. I will tell them to behave. Perhaps Cho-Ko-Ley can cure the boy's fever and we won't have to kill any of them."

"Do you intend to pay court to one of those women? The black one has a nice body, but the yellow-haired mother and daughter are repulsive, even for White Eyes!"

"I think I did a foolish thing back at the wagon, my father. When the black White-Eyed girl spoke to me in Spanish, I told her none of them would be hurt if they did as I said."

Kaya-Tenay frowned thoughtfully at the younger man. "You offered terms? I think that was foolish of you, Eskinya."

"I agree I was a fool, my father. Just the same, in the heat of the moment, I gave my word, and up until now, the captives have obeyed every order I have given them."

Kaya-Tenay sighed and nodded, turning away.

It was too bad, he thought, for the black one had a very nice body indeed and, as chief, she should have been his for the asking. But that young fool had offered terms, and in accepting them, the White Eyes had placed themselves under Eskinya's protection. No woman, with any kind of body, was worth a fight to the death with a man as deadly as Eskinya. So thin-skinned as his son was about his honor as a man, he'd probably even fight to save that ugly woman's ugly children!

THE PRAIRIE SCHOONER lay on its side, two wheels off the ground like the legs of a dead cow. The canvas top had been torn from the hoops and draped over a clump of cholla. The contents of the wagon bed were scattered across the surrounding desert as if some very large and very boisterous children had tipped over a toy box and rummaged through it thoughtlessly, before running off to another place to play.

The team had been run off and there were no bodies near the wagon, so Matt Caldwell was able to sit his camel as he circled the overturned wagon, staring soberly down at the desert pavement. He spotted hoof marks and called out, "Here! I've got tracks running off to the south!"

Greenberg, on the other side of the wagon, called back, "I got some headed north. Tracks don't mean shit this close to where they've hit." As Caldwell circled to join Greenberg and Trooper Dorfler on the north side of the wagon, Trooper Mulvany to the east called out, "Two ponies headed off due east, Lieutenant!"

Greenberg nodded and told Caldwell, "That's how Apaches leave the field, Lieutenant. They wiped this party out and took off in ever' direction, like the spokes of a wagon wheel. They likely drug the other bodies to the four corners as they went, jest to puzzle us a mite."

The scout spit downwind and added, "Later on, they'll have jined up, someplace they picked out ahead of time. We'uns is supposed to waste half a day trackin' in ever' direction whilst them rascals put some miles betwixt themselves and ussen."

Caldwell saw that Rabbit-Boss, poking through the debris on foot, had found something. He called out to the Digger, and Rabbit-Boss held up a small buckskin bag the size of a goose egg. Greenberg spit again and explained, "That's a four-pollen pouch. Supposed to be heap big medicine. These folks run into Apache right enough."

"That thing's an Apache fetish?"

"Don't know what a fetish might be, but that's a four-pollen pouch right enough. Don't have to look inside to savvy it's filled with corn pollen, squash pollen, bean pollen, and tobacco pollen. It's a fool idear they picked up offen the Pueblos. Apache set a heap of store in crosses, too. They say Mangas Coloradas wears a big gold crucifix he took offen a dead Mexican priest after the Battle of Santa Rita. Apaches kilt priests in that one. Rode off all gussied up in crosses and them silver religious medals the Mexicans wear."

Rabbit-Boss had dropped the pollen bag and picked up a girl's petticoat. He held it at arm's length, dropped it, and opined, "Small squaw. Not old enough yet."

"My God!" gasped Caldwell. "They've taken a white girl!"

Greenberg shrugged and said, "That's usually what you'll find in an immigrant wagon. Be a bigger surprise iffen he'd found an Injun gal's shimmy shirt, wouldn't it?"

Caldwell swung around in his saddle and called out, "Corporal Muller! Dismount the men and have them police the entire area. I want everyone to be on the lookout for any scrap of paper they may find. I want to know who these people in this wagon might have been."

He saw his orders were being carried out and knelt his own camel to dismount. He walked over to where Rabbit-Boss was rummaging through a broken box and asked, "Do you think this was a family party, Rabbit-Boss?"

The Indian said, "I think they were big fools. Two men, two women, two children, crossing here alone in daylight. I think this was a bad fight for them. I think Apache must have laughed very much."

"You can read all that in this mess? How do you know they were hit by daylight?"

"They were following old wagon trace. No moon last night, and they did not know this country. Wheel tracks show wagon was rolling until Apache stopped them. If it had been night, the White Eyes would have been camped. Cooking pots taken, but no sign of campfire. My word, I think you must be very blind, even for a Blue Sleeves!"

"I'm trying to learn. How do you know it was two couples and a pair of kids?"

From where he lounged on his own camel, Goldberg called down, "The Injun's right, you're blind as a bat full of Maryland rye! Cain't you *read* them shoe prints all around the wagon, Lieutenant? It's like the fool Injun says, two men, two women, two kids. The kids is a boy of six or eight. Gal's nigh growned, but built light. She's light on her feet as a kid, but she's startin' to walk like a woman. You kin see, over there, where some buck walked her over to a pony and swooped her up and away. The Injun rode southeast with her, but of course, that don't mean a thing."

Caldwell stared at what to him were meaningless scuff marks in the hard-packed gravel. "What about the other women and the younger child? Were they carried in the same direction?".

Greenberg shook his head. "One gal and the kid went off to the north betwixt two Injuns. Other gal was put on a burro and carried west, the way the menfolks' footprints lead."

A trooper searching for sign in that direction called out, "Hey, Lieutenant? I think there's some dry blood on the brush over here!"

Caldwell made a note that Trooper Corrie was a better-than-average observer as Greenberg opined, "That'd be where at least one of 'em bought it, then. I reckon the men was out front with the team and never knowed what hit 'em. Had they drawed blood as the Apache come in agin' 'em, they'd have kilt the whole lot. I suspicion it was a clean ambush and Diablito was in a good mood, fer an Apache, I mean."

"You think the women and children may still be alive?"

"Fer now mebbe. They wouldn't have wasted time puttin' 'em aboard broncs if all they aimed at was to kill 'em."

"Jesum Crow! I'll bet they've all been raped or worse by now!"

Greenberg spit again. "Well, that's hard to say. Them Mexicans never named Diablito Little Devil 'cause they admired his manners all that much. But Injuns ain't as hell-bent on rape as some folks reckon. I'd say a lot depends on how good-lookin' them white gals is, and how willin' they is to let themselves *be* raped."

"You mean, they're liable to have a choice?"

"Well, that depends on what sort of hombres has them. I mean, you take an Injun gal, captured by white men . . . What would you say the chances of her gettin' raped was?"

"Well, I don't know. It would depend a lot on what sort of white men were holding her and . . . Hmmm, I see what you mean. But I thought all Apache were pretty savage."

"Oh, they're savage right enough. Not too many hombres kin hold a candle to an Apache fer bein' savage. But I'd say most men, red or white, would ruther have a gal come willin' to his bedroll. These two white gals might be too skeered to see that. Lots of times when a gal says Injuns raped her, she really means she was skeered to say no, or too lazy to gather firewood when she could be the pet of some big

hoorah. As fer the kids, most Injuns is good to kids.
Apaches has adopted so dern many Mexican kids, the
tribe's half spic by now!"

Rabbit-Boss, having completed his examination of
the surroundings, had squatted in the shade of the
overturned wagon and closed his eyes.

Caldwell went over to him and asked, "Which trail
do you think we should travel, Rabbit-Boss?"

The Indian didn't bother to open his eyes as he
answered, "Every sign false trail. Greenberg right, my
word. The Snakes have ridden off all over, to meet
over that way and ride through night."

Caldwell saw the Digger had pointed to the north
with his chin, and asked, "You think they've ridden
to the north with their captives?"

Rabbit-Boss looked about to fall asleep as he
grunted, "Wee-Tshitz does not *think* they rode north.
Wee-Tshitz *knows* they rode north. Wee-Tshitz has
spoken. You ride any way you like."

"Listen, I'm not questioning your ability, uh, Wheat-
Shit . . ."

"Call me Rabbit-Boss."

"All right, Rabbit-Boss, I just wanted to know how
you could tell which way they'd gone."

Rabbit-Boss opened his eyes and stared thoughtfully up at the younger man. "Hear me, Blue Sleeves,
this land you do not understand was made in the days
of Hohokam by . . . Lord Grizzly."

Rabbit-Boss leaned forward and began to claw the
gravel with his fingers in a north-to-south direction as
he explained, "When Lord Grizzly made this land, he
clawed it so. He left it as it is today, with many many
mountain ranges running like *this,* do you see?"

"Yes, long fault-block ridges running north and
south with wide, flat desert basins between them. We
have much of this on our ordnance map, Rabbit-Boss."

"I have seen the map the man called Fremont
made. Your Fremont was a great fool. The ranges and
flats are all in the wrong places. But hear me, there

are different ways of living in this country. My people live one way. Apache and other Snakes must live another. Do you know how one finds water for a pony in this country?"

"We have most of the wells and seasonal streams mapped out and . . ."

"You do not know how to find water. You do not know how to *live* in my country!"

"All right, suppose I don't. We were talking about Diablito and where you think he might be going."

"He must take the middle way, between the path of my people and the path of the Snakes. If he follows the ridges, where there is grass and water, he will run into other Snakes. The ones you call Bannock or Shoshoni. If he gets too far out on the flats, there will be no fodder, and such water as there may be, after a rain, is bad water."

"In other words, they have to skirt along the edges of the north-south ridgeways, riding by night and skulking in a draw during daylight."

"Now you have started to listen instead of buzzing in my ear like a fly. The fastest travel in this country is always north and south, and Diablito will want to travel fast after hitting this wagon so close to fort. If he follows the river valley, he will be seen from the fort and attacked by the dung-grubbing Mojave near the river. So he has one ridge between his people and the river and hopes to slip north to the great emptiness your Fremont named the Devil's Playground. There is another river up that way, a river you do not have on your map. If the Apache can keep their ponies alive that far, they will be safe from you Blue Sleeves, and very few Real People go there."

"I see, but what's the matter with his going south to his own . . ." Then he saw the disgusted look on Rabbit-Boss's face and quickly decided, "He can't go back to his own country. The other Apache are after him. I guess his best bet *would* be a desert hideout no white man knows about. I'm beginning to see how you do it, Rabbit-Boss. You don't track your prey by spotting every footprint it might have left. You use your knowledge of the desert to think ahead to where the man or animal you're following *has* to go!"

"Of course," said the Indian. "Did you think, my word, I was some kind of dog?"

"I think," said Caldwell soberly, "there's more to you and your people than meets the eye, Wheat . . . uh, how *did* you say your name before?"

"Just call me Rabbit-Boss, Blue Sleeves. I savvy what is in your heart. I think you are a good man, but, my word, *dumb!*"

SINCE THE NADENE did not want to be tracked, and since the camel patrol needed light to track by, the second sunset reversed activity for the two sides. Matt Caldwell ordered a halt for the night, after following Rabbit-Boss a little over twelve miles to the north without spotting the true trail of Kaya-Tenay's band. It had been his idea to camp in a clear and sandy wash where their campfires would not be seen, but Rabbit-Boss insisted they form their circle on the rim of the wash and, when pressed, retreated into a sullen silence.

Meanwhile, to the north, the Nadene were breaking camp for another night march. Eskinya placed his captives, riding double, on the mounts of trusted followers. Ernestine Unger was ordered to ride with young Digoon, their weights balanced on Eskinya's injured pony, Hummingbird-Dancer. The lighter Alfrieda rode with Eskinya's friend, Naiche, a stolid, middle-aged Husband who liked children. The black White-Eyed girl, Jezebel, was told to ride behind Eskinya on his favorite mount, Feet-with-Wings. When Jezebel explained the strange weeping and wailing of the other woman as concern for her son's whereabouts, Eskinya explained, "He is riding with my mother, Cho-Ko-Ley. He must be kept warm inside those deerskins, and this night promises to be cold. My mother says she must hold him tightly and listen to his heart with her own until his fever breaks. He will die if his own foolish mother holds him. Cho-Ko-Ley says the three of you were making the wrong medicine. Are there no fevers among your people?"

Jezebel called out to the boy's mother and sister in the waterfowl gabble of the northern White Eyes, and after some argument, the ugly old woman with yellow hair stopped screaming. Eskinya nodded and told Jezebel, "She is bigger than young Digoon and she may think foolish thoughts about overpowering him and getting away. Warn her I have put her on a lame pony with this in mind."

Jezebel replied, "She would never try to escape unless she could take her children with her. She might leave *me,* but not her own flesh and blood."

Eskinya saw the others were moving out and heeled his pony up the bank of the wash, as Jezebel, frightened by the sudden lunges of Feet-with-Wings, clung tightly to the Indian youth's naked waist. They reached the even level to the north, and as the pony's gait became more reassuring, the captive Jezebel flushed warmly and released her death grip, keeping only one hand lightly on Eskinya's breechclout band. It was hard to touch the fool Injun without touching bare flesh, and Jezebel felt embarrassed enough riding astride like a he-nigger. She'd tried to sit sidesaddle, like a well-brought-up serving girl from a quality house, but the man she rode with had laughed and insisted she ride "sensibly," and do Jesus, her skirts were above her naked knees!

It was too dark to see the legs of Mizz Ernestine and Mizz Frieda, but Jezebel just knew these Injuns had made them ride the same improper way. Once, when she spotted Mizz Frieda riding nigh, she was tempted to warn her to keep her skirts as close to her ankles as she could, but she knew there were things a darky had to watch out about bringing up to white folks.

The Nadene rode in an alternating series of jolting trots and briefer walks to rest their mounts. From the frightened memories of the night before, Jezebel knew they seldom stopped to stretch their legs or relieve themselves, and she sincerely hoped, as she bounced along on the thin blanket between her exposed groin and this awful pony's sharp spine, that her kidneys wouldn't betray her. She'd never in this world be able to up and ask this Injun she was riding with to stop along the way. The less they talked about her female parts the better. She'd been raped once by a white man back in Georgia. It had been her one and only sexual experience, and she had no intention of repeating it any sooner than she had to.

After a time, the column slowed to a walk and Eskinya, in Spanish, asked the captive behind him, "What did you mean about the yellow-haired woman leaving you behind? What relation of hers are you?"

Jezebel blinked in surprise. "Relation? How could we be related? Can't you see I'm *black?*"

Eskinya said, "Of course. You are a black White Eyes, what the Mexicans call a *gringa negra,* but you were traveling together. Are you not of the same band?"

"I *belong* to Señora Unger, if that is what you mean. I am her slave."

The Spanish word for "slave" was unfamiliar to Eskinya, and Jezebel tried other words she knew until they'd settled on "captive."

The Indian nodded. "Now I understand. These White Eyes took you in a fight with your people. Have they adopted you, or are you still free to get away if you can?"

Jezebel shook her head. "You don't understand at

all. Señora Unger didn't capture me. My grandparents were captured long ago in another country. These people bought me from . . . Oh my, it is hard to explain, speaking Spanish to an Apache!"

"Why do you call me your enemy? Are you still angry because we had to kill those men back at the wagon? You told me this afternoon the men we killed were not kinsmen of yours or the yellow-haired people."

Jezebel tried to understand, but the mixture of bad Spanish and strange Indian terms didn't make much sense. She said, "I don't want you to be our enemy. I don't want to be anybody's enemy. I only want to be allowed to go on living!"

Eskinya was aware of the sob in her voice, and his voice was gentle as he soothed, "I have spoken to my father and the others. None of my people will hurt you as long as you behave. I think my mother likes the boy called Willy. It has been a long time since she had young children of her own. Maybe she will adopt him if he does not die. White Eyes do not make very good Nadene, but such things have happened."

Not understanding, Jezebel said nothing.

They rode in silence for a time. Then Eskinya said, "I am a Husband. I have been on many raids and I have six ponies and two burros. One of the ponies, the one I told you about, has a bad leg. The others are all fine animals."

"That's nice. Which of those Apache ladies is your wife, the pretty one with the red ribbons in her braids?"

"That would be my sister, Lu-Ka. She is the wife of Naiche, who has the yellow-haired girl on his pony. I have no wife. I used to have a wife, but she was killed by Mexicans near Jano. That was a bad fight we had at Jano."

"Oh, then you mean you *used* to be a Husband."

"No. Once a boy has fought well four times, he is always a Husband, whether he has a wife or not. I think when we have reached safer camp grounds, I may take another wife. A wife is a lot of trouble, but there are things to be said for having one. Were you ever married, in the country black White Eyes come from?"

"No," said Jezebel. "Slaves, I mean, captives like me don't get married. Our masters sometimes let us say we're married, but it's not the same thing. No woman can be married to a man who doesn't own his own body, can she?"

"Your words are very strange. The White Eyes must have customs very different than ours. How long have you been a captive, anyway?"

"You mean before you captured me? All my life. I was born a captive and I suppose I'll die a captive. Some of the White Eyes, as you call them, have said it's wrong to keep my people the way they do, but the ones who own black people will never let them go without a fight."

"I see. Your people must have done a very bad thing to the White Eyes. When my people hate captives, they kill them."

"What . . . what happens if someone like me is captured by Indians who don't hate her?"

"After you have been with us a while, and we see you know how to act, you might be adopted by some older woman who has no children, or one of the Husbands will ask you to marry him."

Jezebel gasped, "You must be joking. We've heard the way Indians treat captured women. You're only playing cat and mouse with us, aren't you?"

"I do not know this game. You and the others are small and helpless. If we intended you any harm, we would have done it by now."

"You mean you don't torture prisoners?"

"Of course we torture prisoners, if we hate them. But why should we hate you, or the others we took from the wagon? Were any of our people hurt? Have you, the ugly old woman, or either of the children done anything bad to us? Truly, you speak very foolish words, even for a woman. Maybe if I taught you to speak Nadene, you would make more sense. The tongue of the Mexicans is as foolish as the people who speak it. They, too, speak all the time of hate and torture. The Jesus Ghost they say lives in the sky must be a very cruel person."

They rode a time in silence. Then Jezebel asked, "How do you say hello in Apache?"

"You say *nil deesh-ash,* and you do not call us Apache. We are Nadene, Real People. Is this so hard to understand?"

Jezebel twisted her lips around the unfamiliar sounds and managed, "Neal dish-ash. Naw, is that hello, Real Person?"

Eskinya laughed, and the captive girl was surprised how much an Apache laughed like other folks, both black and white, as he explained, "There is no way to say hello, as your people mean it. When a Real Person meets another, and they do not think the other wants to fight, they say nothing, or perhaps they say what is happening. What you just said means that you are coming with me, and this is true."

"I suppose it is." She frowned, then giggled and repeated, "Neal dish-ash, Eskimo. That is your name, isn't it, Eskimo?"

Eskinya laughed again and said, "That is better than Apache. I teach you to speak our language and then you will be . . . I am not sure. Would you like to be a black Nadene, or do you wish to remain as you are, a black White Eyes?"

Jezebel didn't answer, and after a time Eskinya said, "I asked you a question."

The slave girl answered, "I know. I'm thinking about my answer."

ANOTHER RACIAL DISCUSSION was taking place a day's ride to the south, as the men of Caldwell's camel patrol made camp for the night. The argument was between Troopers Streeter and Rogers, the only native-born enlisted men, aside from Corporal Muller, who preferred to chew his tobacco in lofty silence as he lounged against his saddle. At the suggestion of Rabbit-Boss, there was no fire. The camels had been allowed to graze their cuds and belch contentedly to one another in the darkness. The men were fed cold pemmican and hardtack, washed down with warm canteen water. The wiser hands among them had thought to spice their water with a few drops of vinegar, but even so, it was easy enough to heed the corporal's warning to go easy on the stale water.

The lukewarm argument between Streeter and Rogers was political, and the immigrants listened with little interest. Rogers was a New Englander and Streeter was a poor white from the Carolinas. Neither Streeter nor any member of his hard-working family had ever had the thousand dollars for one slave, but to Streeter, the "peculiar institution" was a point of personal honor. He seemed willing to defend with his life, not the possession of a black man, but his sacred right to possess one if he ever got the chance.

Rogers, who had never been in Dixie, was just as adamant in his own religious conviction that all men were brothers—Apaches, Mexicans, and Trooper Streeter being possible exceptions. When Streeter repeated his suggestion that slavery was a just punishment for the black descendants of Cain, Rogers asked innocently, "Don't you think your own family might have come down from Adam and Eve, Streeter? I mean, you don't *look* that much like a monkey, but . . ."

Streeter fell into the trap by snorting, " 'Course my folks come down from Adam and Eve. Ever'body comes from Adam and Eve, goddamn it! What are you, some kinda cotton-pickin' heathen?"

"I was just wonderin', seein' as you think Adam and Eve was colored folk."

"Colored folk? Adam and Eve? Now who in thunder ever said a fool thing like that?"

"You did. You said Cain was a nigger, born to be your slave. If Cain was a nigger, and his ma was Eve, and his pa was Adam . . ."

"Oh, Jesus, you are purely stupid, Yankee! I never said Cain was no nigger. I said his *chillens* was! It says so right in the Good Book. It says how Cain kilt his own brother and was sent to live all by his lonesome off in the Land of Nod."

"Yeah? Well, how did his kids get to be black, then?"

"Well, do Jesus, there warn't no *folks* in the Land of Nod, were there?"

"I dunno. It says he went into the Land of Nod until he came to a City of Men."

"Don't be an idjet! The onliest men was back home with Adam and Eve and the rest of us white folks. The folks Cain met up with was somethin' else. No decent white gal was about to marry up with Cain, after the way Cain done his own kin! The onliest way Cain could have chillens was to marry up with some sort of monkey gal, or mebbe some breed of ape. Anyway, he married *somethin'* over there in Nod, and them niggers you keep frettin' over is what come outten Cain's loins. The Good Lord spared Cain's life, instead of hangin' him, so's decent folks would have niggers to help 'em with their chores."

Rogers snorted. "That's stupid. Colored people are children of God, just like you and me!"

"Oh yeah? Then how'd they git so goddamn dumb and black? Anyone with eyes to see can tell a nigger ain't quite human."

"All right, let's say they're different, for the sake of this fool argument. Let's say the Lord made more than one kind of man, or even a critter that ain't quite a man. That still don't give you the call to treat those folks so mean, does it?"

"Shoot, I ain't never been mean to no nigger in my life. Niggers don't *mind* workin' for a white man. Why, I've seen niggers back home jest singin' and laughin' all day whilst they chopped cotton or split a few cords of wood."

"Is that a fact? How come you have to lick 'em with a whip, or chase 'em down with bloodhounds, if they're all so happy about bein' slaves?"

"Now listen, damn it, you're jest talkin' 'bout a lot of things no Yankee understands, you hear?"

Lounging nearby, Matt Caldwell was aware of the angry edge the Southern boy's voice was taking on, and murmured, "Corporal?" to his noncom, Muller. Muller spit, said, "Yes, sir," and in a louder tone called, "Streeter? I think you'd better relieve Csonka out on the picket. That fool Polack can't see as good as you in the dark."

Streeter muttered, "Damn Yankees don't have sense to find their own assholes in the latrine!" as he got to his feet and moved out under the stars, shouting, "Hey, Csonka, where the hell you at?"

Caldwell was aware that Muller had favored his fellow Northerner in breaking up the dispute, but it was the New Yorker's squad, and a good officer backed his noncoms as far as possible.

At least the others hadn't taken sides in this stubborn dispute that was tearing the Regular Army to bits. There had been fistfights among the enlisted men and whispered talk of secret duels among certain hot-

headed junior officers. One congressman had beaten
another unconscious with his cane right in the House
Of Representatives, and if that new Republican Party
actually tried to put an Abolitionist in the White
House in the coming election, there was no telling
what might happen. Those Southern threats of taking
thirteen states out of the Union were preposterous,
but it did seem sinister, the way Secretary Davis had
managed to put so many of his own in key positions.
Those guns they'd ordered out of Leavenworth to bol-
ster a Texas garrison made little sense, with the border
quiet and the Comanche behaving themselves again.
That officer he'd warned about seditious talk back east
was probably just enamored of the sound of his own
voice, but that talk about loyalty to one's own state
coming ahead of any oath he'd given to the Union
had come perilously close to out-and-out treason.
What had that fool's name been? Oh, yes, Stuart.
J. E. B. Stuart. The other Southerons called the hot-
head "Jeb." Someone had threatened to send a letter
about him through channels, but of course, nobody
had. The army washed its own dirty linen, and if the
Kiowa didn't kill Jeb Stuart, he'd probably grow up
before that talk about states' rights got him in any serious trouble.

His chain of thought was broken by Digger Greenberg coming over to hunker down beside him. The
scout bit off a chaw from the inexhaustible supply of
cut plug he seemed to have and muttered, "We ain't
all that fer from Fort Havasu. Make in a few hours,
did we ride whilst cool and comfortable like."

Caldwell said, "Those Apache have white women
and children with them. Rabbit-Boss says they'll be
making forty or fifty miles a night. We can do sixty
if we have to, and . . ."

"Back up, I never said we had to leave them folks
with them Apache, Lieutenant. I only aim to swing
over to the fort, pick up at least a full platoon,
and . . ."

"I don't want to waste the time. Besides, I'm not sure Captain Lodge would give me the extra men. He's just as likely to hold us all at Havasu and send to Fort Yuma for reinforcements. You know he's holding that crossing with a skeleton force, as it is."

"Well, what iffen he does take us offen them rascals' trail? It ain't our fault them fool immigrants tried to cross back there alone, is it?"

"Damn it, Goldberg, those women and children are depending on us!"

"No, they ain't. They don't know we'uns is followin' after Diablito like the idjets we is!"

Caldwell allowed his lip to curl as he suggested, "If you're so frightened, why don't you just ride on back to the fort alone?"

The scout spit. "I ain't been hired to do that. Me an' Rabbit-Boss is drawin' three dollars a day to lead you jaspers wherever in tarnation you think you're aimin' fer."

"Well, I'm aiming to catch Diablito and rescue the captives."

"Shit, you ain't about to do no sech thing. I keep tryin' to tell you them Apache outnumber us four or five to one. You jest figure to keep followin' that ornery Diablito till he *catches* you!"

"Trained troops have been a match for ten-to-one Indians in the past. Why, at Medicine Wells . . ."

"Goddamn it, we ain't talkin' 'bout Injuns! We're talkin' 'bout *Apache!* You think Diablito's about to hit us whoopin' and a-wailin' like a mess of crazy Sioux? Sioux fight out in the open, like we'uns."

"All right, how do Apache fight?"

"You jest keep this foolishness up, sonny, and I suspicion you'll likely find out the hard way."

KAYA-TENAY RODE AHEAD of his people, singing softly to the stars. His pony was a good one and the night was cool. The northern constellation his people called Nahukos circled the One Star That Never Moves as faithfully as ever, and it was good to be alive.

Though Rabbit-Boss was sure the wanderers were making for the Mojave River, Kaya-Tenay had no idea just where he was taking his people. The ranges and basins were much the same up this way as they had been in the Sonora Desert, and he knew vaguely that lesser peoples inhabited this new land. If they stayed out of his way, Kaya-Tenay bore them no ill will. If there was no good water up ahead, he would simply ride until they came to some. Meanwhile, the ponies could manage on prickly pear, once the women and children gathered some and peeled it for the ponies' tender muzzles. His principal wife, Cho-Ko-Ley, said they had enough food for the next few days. Maybe, when he was certain no Blue Sleeves were following, he would lead a hunt up the nearest ridge. At this time of the year, there would be plenty of game in the high country. Tonight he would simply enjoy life.

Kaya-Tenay smiled at the North Star and sang:

"The father of the night, he stirs.
Among the dancing little eyes of night, he stirs.
Among the flying bats and owls, he stirs.
The pollen of the night-blooming cactus flowers, he stirs.
He stirs, he stirs, he stirs, he stirs!"

His song went on like this for many verses, and to a white person, it might have sounded monotonous. To Kaya-Tenay, it was beautiful, for four is a good number and all good things should be repeated four times.

Had Kaya-Tenay possessed a modern map, or had he known the Great Basin as well as Rabbit-Boss, he would have been leading his people more to his left. The Mojave River has its beginnings in the San Bernadino Range far to the west of Kaya-Tenay's chosen route. Like other rivers of the Great Basin, the Mojave has no outlet to the sea. It runs down cool and clear from the snow-capped San Bernardinos, winds north and east across nearly a hundred miles of bone-dry desert, and slowly dies in a vast inland delta of treacherous tule marsh and seasonal lakes and salt flats. It was into this land of low-lying desert marsh that Kaya-Tenay was taking his people.

Such water as there was was a bitter poisonous brew of potash, borax, sodium chloride, and other salts. Nothing lived in what the Diggers called the Big Emptiness, for the soil was poisoned, too, and nothing moved across the barren playas of sun-baked mud or dazzling salt but drifting sand and the occasional shadow of a soaring buzzard. Sometimes, foolish mustangs or an occasional lost antelope fawn wandered out into the Big Emptiness, and a hungry buzzard sometimes took a chance on finding a meal along the edges of the vast expanse. One day white men would map the stretch between Death Valley and the Colorado, and one day twenty-mule teams would haul borax from the hellish flats, but they would fight no Indians for possession of this dead heart of the desert. No Indians who knew the Great Basin ever went there. Kaya-Tenay would not have gone there, had he known what Nahukos and the other stars were leading him into.

A quail called from the darkness ahead. Kaya-Tenay answered with the soft yip of a kit fox, and the shadowy form of a mounted scout materialized against

the starlit north horizon. Kaya-Tenay had sent his
nephew, Poinsenay, ahead of the column to make sure
there were no ghosts or other strangers waiting in ambush out there in the darkness. There were other Husbands, of course, fanned out ahead and to either side
of the column, so Kaya-Tenay didn't stop his followers
as he rode to join Poinsenay. The way was still secure, or the recognition signal would have been the
sound of Brother Coyote, barking a warning to his
mate. Poinsenay would say, in his own good time, why
he'd dropped back.

The two men rode side by side for a time. Then
Poinsenay said, "There is nothing out there ahead of
us. Once, I saw what looked like a Spirit Bear rearing
up against the sky. It was only one of those yucca trees
they have in this country. I have been seeing less and
less cactus and more and more of the shaggy yucca
trees."

Kaya-Tenay nodded. "I have noticed. Country always changes as one moves about. I think this is a
good thing. There would be no point in wandering if
the country everywhere was the same. If every hill
and valley was the same, nobody would ever travel
and the whole world would live as Pueblos and Mexicans do!"

Kaya-Tenay grimaced, and then, because he considered himself a fair-minded man, he said, "I take
that back. Mexicans move about a little. Even they
must wonder sometimes what lies over the faraway
ridges. The Pueblos are the ones I do not understand.
Can you imagine yourself being born, living all your
life, and lying down for the Long Sleep, without ever
having left the same canyon?"

Poinsenay said, "No. There is something else I
noticed up ahead. The hills to either side are spreading wider, ever wider, like the jaws of a great coyote.
Only, we are riding *out*, not in, and this basin grows
ever wider and more open as we go north."

"What of it? No two basins are the same in detail,

yet all in the end are not too different. As this one opens here, it has to close there. There is a valley beyond each hill and, beyond each valley, a hill. I was told this long ago by my father's father, and I have always found this to be true."

Poinsenay was silent for a time. Then he said, "It is very quiet out there. I do not think it is the silence of living things that freeze in the night because a man moves among them. I think it is so quiet because there is nothing there!"

"There is always something there, nephew. This is the dry time of the summer before the rains, and the basins are nearly empty of game, but . . ."

"Forgive me if I speak before you have spoken, uncle, but this is important!"

"It must be! What is the matter with you? Why are you afraid of a few yucca trees and the absence of a few crickets?"

"I do not know. I think there may be a witch among us. Something is crawling around inside my scalp near the back of my neck. I began to think, as I rode the point out front, that I was somehow riding *downhill.*"

"That is not possible. The Colorado runs into the Sea of Cortez to the south, and we have hardly risen above the level of the Colorado's banks since we crossed it. We have skirted the easy ridge routes and kept to the dry flats. If this basin was taking us downhill, it would mean we were going lower than the level of the Great Bitter Sea, and this, my nephew, is impossible."

"I know. I had other feelings out there alone in the darkness. I began to feel eyes, unfriendly eyes, and far far away, I seemed to hear someone, or some *thing,* laughing at us. I think, my uncle, we should turn back! I think the trail ahead is bad!"

Kaya-Tenay said, "There are no friends back the way we came. I have been in bad country before. Always, I have found better country on the other side. You may take your women and ponies back if you are afraid. If you tell Nana you are now my enemy, I do not think he will do more than shame you a little."

Poinsenay didn't answer. Kaya-Tenay hadn't expected him to. They rode on for a time in silence as the older man considered his nephew's suspicions of witchcraft. Like most Indians, the Nadene lived in a world devoid of accident. Where a white person might consider the unexpected misfortune a random fall of the cosmic dice, Kaya-Tenay knew that everything in life happened for a reason. Enemies struck at him because they were enemies. The sidewinder bit a child or pony because it was a snake, and snakes were meant to do such things. He understood the miss of an arrow to be the poor aim of the man with the bow, and when a pony drank bad water and died, he sensed this as the mistake of a foolish rider. Beyond these obvious avoidable dangers, his universe was peopled by evil forces only ghosts and sorcerers fully understood. Sickness and other misfortunes a man could do nothing much about were caused by some offended spirit, or the secret spells of a treacherous enemy. There *did* seem to be something wrong out there in the darkness. Something that reminded him of another time the spirit world had seemed to close in around him.

Kaya-Tenay said, "Once, when I was a boy, we hunted bighorn in a canyon where the Anasazi had lived long ago, before our people came up into this world from the Caves of Creation."

"I know the place, my uncle. The long-dead Anasazi dwelt there in their stone wickiups, up among the ledges of the canyon walls."

"That is the canyon I mean. The Pueblos say that once, when the world was younger and greener, the Anasazi grew corn and even squash among the bone-dry rocks of their haunted canyons, but the day we hunted there, not a twig of saltbush could be found. There was no water and the canyon was silent. There were no lizards among the rocks. We lost the trail of the bighorn we'd been tracking, and when we stopped to consider where it might have gone, there were not even flies around our ponies' droppings. Truly, the long-dead Anasazi had that canyon to themselves."

"It is a bad place," his nephew agreed. "I have heard it said the Anasazi sit there, dried like jerky, staring down with empty eye sockets from the caves in the canyon walls. They say that once a Mexican disturbed the Anasazi there, searching for the Yellow Iron they like so much. They say the Mexican came down from the canyon, wide-eyed and frightened by something he saw in one of those caves. Some Real People found him, wandering in a mad daze and dying of thirst. Since he was mad, they did not wish to kill him, but he died anyway, screaming like an animal. He said, before he died, that evil bats had bitten him, but of course, that was only what the ghosts of the dead Anasazi wished him to believe. Did you see evil bats that day, my uncle?"

"No. We did not go into the caves or stone wickiups. But we only felt the dead around us. My brother said he thought we should leave the canyon. The rest of us agreed. It felt wrong to be in such a place alive." He hesitated and added, "It felt as it does now! I think what we feel in the night around us is not witchcraft. I think this country stinks of death!"

"I think so, too. Are we going to turn back or, at least, go *around* this basin?"

Kaya-Tenay slowed his pony and stared up at the stars as he mused, "It may be better if we swing closer to the mountains, but I am not sure whether we should go east or west. The stars tell only north from south. They don't say which range has the most water. I think we shall keep this path until morning gives me a better view of the peaks. It would be foolish to ride out of our way into mountains too low for good hunting and grazing."

Suiting action to his words, Kaya-Tenay heeled his pony onward with renewed confidence, saying, "You had better take that point again. Ride toward that bright yellow star on the . . . on the horizon . . . ?"

Both men reined their ponies in as the possible meaning of what they saw in the distance sank in. Neither spoke for a time. Then Poinsenay said, "Uncle, I do not think that is a star. I think that is a campfire."

Kaya-Tenay nodded soberly. "I think you are right."

THE TEN AMERICAN prospectors and their two Mexican guides were worried as they sat around their campfire, discussing the route they intended to follow in the morning. Their worry was not about Indians, since no Indians roamed this part of the Great Basin, except for a few miserable Diggers too meek to consider attacking such a large force of armed white men. The party had struck out into the desert from the picked-over gold fields east of Los Angeles City, aiming for a vaguely located range called the Panamints. The gold was said to lie like pebbles in the dry stream beds of the Panamints, and it was somewhere this side of Death Valley, but up to now, the Panamints had been a little hard to find, and their water was running low.

The rag-tag band of adventurers were too far south, but they were unaware of this. They only knew the desert was getting hotter and more barren with every mile, and some of them were offering the not-too-impossible suggestion that they were lost. Their nominal leader, a burly Ohio-bred giant called Calico, was for pressing on in the morning. To every suggestion that they might have taken a few wrong turns around a playa, Calico's reply was always the same. Jed Smith had crossed the Mojave back in the twenties, and he, Calico, was just as good a man as any goddamn fool named Jedediah!

When someone pointed out Jed Smith had reported no gold in the desert after making his epic trek to the then-Mexican Pueblo de los Angeles, Calico's ready answer was, "They didn't know about the gold in Californee in them days. Jed Smith and them other Astorians was lookin' fer beaver!"

Someone muttered, "Beaver? In this God-forsaken desert?" and Calico said triumphantly, "I told you boys the man was an idjet, didn't I? I mean, if a man fool enough to hunt beaver in the Mojave kin cross it, I reckon folks as smart as us should make it easy."

The argument went on, getting nowhere, as the men sat around the fire, chewing their plugs and staring morosely into the flames of greasewood roots. It was a large fire, for the night was bitterly cold, and few white men knew the Diggers' trick of keeping warm between two small fires, rather than roasting one side and freezing the other next to a roaring blaze.

Under normal circumstances, the talk around the campfire would have slowly died away as one man after the other stretched out under a blanket on the desert pavement. But this was not a night like any of the others the party had spent on the trail since they'd left the green San Bernardinos.

The only warning was the nervous whinny from one of their hobbled ponies as it sensed a movement in the darkness beyond the circle of the campfire's glow. One of the men stood up, muttering, "somethin' pesterin' my hoss," and then he seemed to freeze in place, staring down at the feathered shaft of the arrow that had just thunked into his chest.

Calico was the first to come unstuck, yelling, "Injuns!" as he rolled to one knee with a buffalo gun in his hands. Two arrows took him over the heart as he fired blindly into the dark, and then he fell back dead across the fire.

From the darkness, a voice shouted, *"Nleidi!"* and another man who'd reached his rifle fell across it face down with three arrows in his back. The others fared little better, though some managed to get off a shot before they died, and two, unfortunately for them, were taken alive when the Nadene swept into the camp on foot.

Only one of Kaya-Tenay's people had been hit. A lucky round had torn the top off Poinsenay's head as he and the others made the final charge. The two captives were to learn, as others had in the past, that one should either kill every member of a Nadene band, or none at all.

MATT CALDWELL WAS awakened at dawn by the frightened voice of a picket shouting, "Corporal of the guard! Post number two!" and the sound of what seemed to be a railroad train roaring by at full steam.

The lieutenant rolled out from under his blanket and jumped to his feet with six-gun in hand. The eastern sky was glowing pearly rose, and the scene around him was just visible in the ruby horizontal light. Matt ran toward the sentry and the railroad sound in the dry-wash bed beyond and stopped wide-eyed as he saw what all the fuss was about. A trooper stopped beside him, gasped, and shouted above the roar, "Jesus Christ!"

The wash was filled nearly to the brim by a swirling, churning flood of muddy water. Even as they watched, the waters rose and they could see piñon trees, juniper logs, and boulders the size of their camels rolling end over end in the liquid mass.

Digger Greenberg and High Jolly walked over to join the growing crowd at the edge of the wash. Greenberg spit thoughtfully into the flash flood and said, "That happens sometimes this late in summer."

Caldwell said, "I owe one to Rabbit-Boss. If it had been up to me, we'd have camped down in that wash last night!"

"Well, that's why I put up with the fool Injun," nodded Greenberg. "He does git notions, but sometimes it pays to listen to the old heathen."

"I see what you mean, but where in hell did all that water come from? There's not a cloud in the sky and . . ."

"Musta rained in the high country last night. That range a dozen miles or so to our west looks high enough to trip a thunderhead."

Caldwell stared at the still-dark west horizon and said, "I think I see some hills over there, but a dozen miles?"

"Shoot, I've seen a flash flood run thirty or more across the flats, with the sun shinin' hot enough to fry an aig and ever' clump of saltbush dried out dead. Gener'ly, they stick to the washes, but a man kin git in lots of trouble on a salt flat this time of the year. Lots of them old flats and playas would be lake bottoms anywheres else in the states." He spit again. "That's the trouble with this danged country. You either gits no water at all, or you gits too blamed much all at once!"

"Remind me never to camp in a dry-wash, Digger."

"Won't have to. You jest larnt better. Just remember one thing, though; there's no hard and fast rules out here. Gener'ly, the water runs down the wash, but a four-foot wall of the shit kin catch you out on a flat, and sometimes a wash kin be a safe hidey hole iffen you know how to read the lay of the land."

"I'm afraid I don't follow you, Digger. Are you saying there are times a man out here might want to camp in a wash?"

"Well, sure, if he's lookin' to hide and knows which ones is safe."

"How can any wash be safe? Just look at that damn water running by down there! It must be going forty miles an hour!"

"More like sixty. Antelope kin run forty miles an hour, and the flash floods sometimes catch 'em on a playa. The way you tell a wash is safe, though, is by the brush along the bottom. Crack willow and old dried tule means a wash gits swept by flash floods regular. No grass and lots of overgrowed mesquite means a wash has oxbowed its fool self dry and ain't gittin' too much water anymore."

Caldwell remembered the oxbow lakes along the Missouri and understood how a shift of channel could cut a section of these smaller stream beds off from the main channel from the mountains. He asked Greenberg, "Why mesquite?" and the scout explained, "Mesquite roots deep. Cain't take much floodin', but its roots tap water deep as sixty feet. A young mesquite kin grow most anywhere, but to git old enough to shade a pony under . . ."

"I see what you mean. There's more to botany out here than meets the eye."

"Yep, a man has to keep his eye peeled for more'n man or beast out here. Mistakin' saltbush fer tarweed has been knowed to kill a man."

"Good God, how could that happen?"

"Easy. Saltbush kin grow near a poison water hole. Tarweed cain't. Most immigrants figure to see skeletons around a poison water hole, but sometimes a look-see at the vegetables is all you got to go on."

"Remind me to take a better look at the next clump of tarweed we pass. The camels seem to like the saltbush, though. Do you think it's safe to let them eat it?"

"Sure, there ain't no poison in saltbush. The stuff

jest ain't too particular 'bout its water, is all. It kin grow with good water nigh its roots, but it does better where the other plants is pi'zened off by salts, washin' soda, arsenic, and other shit that settles in the low spots hereabouts."

Caldwell was suddenly aware that nearly every man in his patrol had joined him at the edge of the wash. He turned and snapped, "Spread out and soldier, damn it! We're bunched like raw recruits in a pay line! Where's Corporal Muller?"

The noncom detached himself from the far end of the line, snapped to attention, and called out, "No excuse, sir!"

"All right, get your men properly dispersed and secure the area. We're taking ten for breakfast, and then it's boots and saddles. Are there any questions, Corporal?"

"No, sir! You others, as you were. Chew if you got it, but no mess fires and no smoking in this light. Each man by his mount and ready to move out in exactly ten minutes."

As the men started to shuffle back to their bedrolls, Muller called after them, "That ten minutes includes piss call. Pack up before you stuff your guts!"

Muller shot his officer a guilty smile and Caldwell nodded, saying, "Carry on, Corporal. I took a bit of time getting the sand out of my eyes, didn't I?"

"If you say so, sir. I won't act such a fool again."

High Jolly left to tend the camels, but Digger Greenberg only seemed amused. He fell in beside Caldwell, walking back to where he'd left his own gear, and the officer asked, "Where's Rabbit-Boss?"

"Out earnin' his keep, I reckon. Injuns don't sleep all that much, and he's put out 'cause I been hoorahin' him 'bout not findin' them Apaches fer you."

"I thought we were following them."

"Well, we is and we ain't. Rabbit-Boss allows they headed north, but he ain't found a sign of the tricky bastards that a man could bank on."

"You mean we could be simply running around in circles out here?"

"We ain't runnin' in circles, we's headed for the Mojave River. The trouble, as I see it, is that them Apache *ain't*. I've given Rabbit-Boss another day to cut their trail his way. He don't do it by sundown, I reckon we'd best try mine."

"I didn't know the two of you had a difference of opinion."

"Well, we do. Rabbit-Boss suspicions they headed fer the Mojave, 'cause it'd be stupid to go anywheres else. I keep tryin' to tell him Apache don't think or act like sensible folks, red or white, but I cain't git the fool Digger to see it my way."

"All right, what is your way, Digger?"

The scout spit and said, "Due north. It's the worst damn way a body could head out here in this damn desert. There's not a damn thing betwixt here and the Providence Range but miles and miles and miles. No fodder, no sweet water, no goddamn reason at all fer goin' that way, 'lessen you jest happen to be Apache."

"That sounds crazy to me."

"Well, of course it's crazy! That's how you figure Apache. You think of the dumbest, pi'zen-mean, most ornery thing you kin, and that's what the nearest Apache's likely to be a-doin'!"

"Damn it, Digger, there'd be no sense in Diablito leading his band into the area you describe. If I was Diablito, I'd want to . . ."

"Back off and think a mite on what you're sayin', Lieutenant! Both you and Rabbit-Boss keep makin' the same fool mistake 'bout Diablito! Rabbit-Boss thinks what any sensible Injun would do. You think what a white man with enough sense to matter might do, and both of you are off the mark. Apache ain't dumb. They know, jest as well as you and me and Rabbit-Boss what anyone with sense would do, then they go and do jest the contrary. How do you reckon they've stayed alive this long, with ever'body from the Papago to Horse Utes agin' 'em?"

"By avoiding the obvious?"

"By avoidin' the *possible!* None of these desert tribes is schoolmarms, Lieutenant. A Papago kin track a lizard over rim rock, and a Horse Ute kin live where a rabbit wouldn't want to. Apache steer clear of good water holes, good pasture, and good shade. They'll ride a pony into the ground, walk sixty miles in one night through rough country, and steal fresh mounts. Surround the sons of bitches and they'll slip through your fingers like spooks to shoot you in the back and run off laughin'. Diablito's even had *Apache* out to kill him, and he's still alive, bouncin' around like spit on a hot stove. You think a man like that's about to lead his band beside still waters, like some jasper from the Good Book? I tell you, I *know* where Diablito's goin'! He's takin' his band into the nearest thing to hell he kin find this side of the real thing!"

By now they were back by Caldwell's bedroll. The officer hunkered down to gather his gear together. "I think your idea makes sense. Just how bad is this country to the north you're talking about? Do you think our camels can carry us across it?"

Greenberg shrugged. "Don't know. Never took a camel into the Big Emptiness afore."

"What did you ride up there?"

"Nothin'. Not even my own two feet. I bin around the edges some. Nobody I know of's ever crossed it, fer as I know. Rabbit-Boss says it ain't possible."

"Don't you think he knows what he's talking about?"

"He knows what he's talkin' 'bout. He jest ain't Apache."

A FEW MILES to the northwest, Wee-Tshitz, last of the
Sage-Grouse People, squatted on his heels in the dawn
light, immobile as the joshua tree behind him. His left-
hand fingers braced him against the dew-moist gravel.
His right hand lightly gripped one end of the all-
purpose wand that rested on his shoulder. White people called the wand of Wee-Tshitz a digging stick, but
it was more than that to him. The long-dead hands
of Wovo-Kah, the medicine smith, had fashioned it
with skill from bristle cone wood, gathered with the
proper ceremonies from the sacred hills above the valley white men would one day call the Owens. Many
flints had been retouched as the medicine smith
scraped it into the proper shape. For the wood of bristle cone is hard and must be fashioned slowly and
with respectful love. The long hours of patient labor
had not been wasted. It was a very good wand. It was
nearly as heavy and as strong as iron. It was all a Real
Person needed if he followed The Way.

Wee-Tshitz felt a cramp in one leg and willed it to
stop hurting. The rabbit he was after would be near by
now. The path of the desert hare is circular. It hates
strange landmarks and, once flushed, will run in a
great circle, trying to keep to the territory it knows. If
the hunter is Brother Coyote, or a man who knows the
rabbit's ways, he freezes in the spot he flushed the
rabbit and waits. If he waits long enough, the rabbit
will complete his circle and . . .

There was a faint movement in the cheat grass and
Wee-Tshitz stopped breathing. He saw the rabbit now,
its ears and quivering nose testing its small corner of

the universe as it took another cautious hop along its great circle of flight. The Indian neither moved nor breathed as he waited for the rabbit to move closer. A very long time went by, and then the rabbit in its own turn froze. Wee-Tshitz read its thoughts, and before it could turn and dart away in another variation of its circular flight, he threw his wand.

The well-balanced length of hardwood flew end over end at its small target and struck, as aimed, a little low. The blunt end hit the gravel and the wand bounced, driving its sharp end through the rabbit just behind the shoulders. Wee-Tshitz bounded after it, reaching the squealing rabbit in less than a dozen strides. The Indian grabbed the small beast behind the ears, murmured, "Forgive me, cousin. My need is great," and squeezed. The rabbit died with little pain, and Wee-Tshitz skinned and gutted it with expert fingers, then turned back to join the Blue Sleeves near the camels. He saw the two thin forms that had risen from the greasewood between him and the camp, and stopped to consider them. They were a young man and woman, naked like himself, and armed with nets and digging sticks. The man spoke Wee-Tshitz's language as he said soberly, "That was our rabbit. Are you a Person?"

Wee-Tshitz said, "Yes. I did not see you hidden there. I would not have killed this rabbit had I known you were hunting it."

The man stared hard at the small animal in the other's hand and tried not to show the fear in his voice. "If you have hunger, we shall share our rabbit with you. If you intend to eat it all, you will have to kill me first."

Wee-Tshitz said, "I am bigger than you, but I do not wish to fight you. I think you and your woman have the better claim to this meat. I would not have been hunting had I known Real People lived here."

He held the rabbit out and the woman came to take it while her man guarded her approach with his own cocked wand. The woman was young, and pretty by the standards of her people, but she was very thin, and as he handed her the rabbit, he said, "The skin is over there if you need it. You do not look as if the hunting has been good around here."

The woman, naturally, did not answer. She ran back to her man with the prize, and for the first time the strange Digger smiled. He said, "I think you are a good person. I meant what I said about sharing with you."

Wee-Tshitz said, "I have less need. I am scouting for some Blue Sleeves and they have been feeding me. I desired fresh meat, but I do not really need it. I think there is little enough for the two of you."

The man nodded, tore the rabbit in two, and without further ceremony the couple sat down to devour the raw meat. Wee-Tshitz stood where he was until they'd finished. It did not take long. He waited until the younger man could speak again, before he said, "I am searching for the trail of many Snakes. They have come from the south and have some White Eyes with them. I think they came this way, but I have not found their sign."

The other Digger said, "You are looking in the wrong direction. We crossed the trail of many ponies yesterday." He pointed at the rising sun with his chin. "Their trail lies over that way a half day's walk from here. We did not see the Snakes. Just their sign. When I see pony tracks, I take another path. Why are you scouting for the Blue Sleeves. Are you not afraid of them?"

"The ones I hunt with hunt Snakes. I help them because I think this is a good thing to do. Besides, they give me food and tobacco."

The other said, "I do. not like to be near White Eyes. Once when I was younger, my father and I went near some White Eyes to ask them for tobacco. There were many of them with a lot of wagons, and we had no weapons but our wands, but the women screamed and the men shot my father and I had to run very fast to get away. I have wondered many times why they were so afraid of us.". .

Wee-Tshitz shrugged. "They are strange people, but I think it best to try and get along with them. We can't make friends with the Snakes, and unless we make friends with *someone,* our people will go the way of the Hohokam and be nothing but ghosts. A friend I have among the White Eyes tells me we must become White Eyes ourselves, or else just vanish from the land as the Hohokam did so long ago."

"Perhaps his words are true, but as for me, I would rather be the ghost of a Real Person than some . . . some *thing* like a White Eyes!"

Before the discussion could continue, the Digger woman suddenly hissed in terror, and all three stared at the moving forms she'd spotted to the south. Wee-Tshitz laughed and said, "Those are the Spirit Horses the Blue Sleeves I told you about use instead of ponies."

But the couple were not listening. Both were running away in blind panic, looking for a place to hide from the awful monsters moving up from the south on those long, ungainly legs. Wee-Tshitz stared after them regretfully, for it was good to hear the language of Real People. The couple vanished as they found cover heavy enough to hide in while running in a crouch, and Wee-Tshitz turned and walked to meet the camel patrol.

The officer and Digger Greenberg spotted him, and the column swung to intercept his eastbound path. Greenberg hailed, "Where do you think you're goin', Old Son?" and the Indian pointed into the sunrise, saying, "Over that way. I have found the path Diablito took."

Greenberg grinned. "Hot damn! Where is it, Rabbit-Boss?"

The Indian said, "Half a day's walk. You were right. They mean to cross the Big Emptiness."

Greenberg shot his Indian companion a curious

look, then shrugged and asked Matt Caldwell, "What did I tell you? I *knowed* the rascals was headed that-away!"

Caldwell frowned. "There's something very funny about this. How in hell does Rabbit-Boss know where the trail is if it's over a dozen miles to the east?"

Greenberg said, "It purely beats me, Lieutenant, but iffen he says he's found the trail, he's likely found the trail. Rabbit-Boss don't hardly lie at all, and that's a fact."

Caldwell signaled a column-left and reined in at Greenberg's side, muttering, "I don't understand this at all. I know the Indian's good, but nobody can spot hoofprints a dozen miles away. Do you suppose he saw some dust, or something?"

"Lieutenant. You gotta understand one thing about these here Diggers. They don't *think* things out like you or me. Rabbit-Boss has . . . well, you might call it *medicine*."

"You mean some sort of sixth sense?"

"Yeah, somethin' like that. They git all sorts of feelin's and notions like. Some folks say it's some secret power an Injun's jest birthed with, savvy?"

A few yards ahead, Rabbit-Boss could hear every word. He could have explained his "secret powers" had he wanted to, but he *didn't* want to. None of the Blue Sleeves seemed to know it, but Indians had a sense of humor, too.

THE SUNRISE CAUGHT Kaya-Tenay and his people on a playa, so there was little point in stopping. Kaya-Tenay led them across the dried lake bed with the hearty bravado born of desperation, for morning was the worse possible time to be out in the open on the desert. The air was crisp and clear before the earth had baked enough to make the middle distances shimmer. Nobody looking down on the playa from a ridge would see the silvery illusions of the spirit waters at this hour. They would see a long, ragged line of moving figures, as exposed as ants on the head of a big buckskin drum. The crackled surface of the sun-baked lake bottom was nearly as hard as cement, and Kaya-Tenay could only be grateful that the ponies of his people left few marks and raised no dust as they crossed in search of cover. There were many ponies now, for the *remuda* of the White Eyes they'd surprised around that great foolish fire had been added to Kaya-Tenay's band, along with many rifles, some fine flannel shirts, and six bottles of the brown tequila the northern White Eyes made. There would have been more, but for some reason, Eskinya had started breaking the flat brown bottles and many had been lost before Kaya-Tenay could order him to stop. When he found cover and had the time, Kaya-Tenay intended to drink some of the brown tequila and see if he could have a vision. He found this new land confusing, and a vision or two might teach him to understand it better. The good and evil forces seemed to struggle here in this northern sector of the world. The mountains were higher and more lush than those to the south, but they were much farther apart and the flat lands between them were wider and more frightening to cross. It was hard to tell whether the gods were with you or against you up here. Kaya-Tenay was growing rich in guns and ponies as he led his people, but the ponies and people were hungry and thirsty, and last night Poinsenay had been killed by a medicine shot from a dead man. This was a very frightening thing to think about, but it had to be faced. The ghosts who dwelt in this strange basin had meant that shot as a message. Perhaps if he got gloriously drunk, Kaya-Tenay would understand its meaning.

Near the rear of the column, Eskinya asked the girl who rode behind him, "Why are you so silent? Have I said something to offend you?"

Jezebel didn't answer for a time. Then she asked, "Why did you do those terrible things to that white man back there? You told me you didn't hurt people unless you had to, but you lied to me. Back there last night you acted like an animal!" She frowned and added, "No, I take that back. No animal would have done the things you did to that poor man with your knife!"

Eskinya said, "I only did what I had to. Poinsenay was my kinsman and they killed him. I only opened him up a little so that Poinsenay's wife and children could get at his entrails. It would have taken him much longer to die, had we left him and the other one entirely to the women and children."

"That's no excuse for what you did. Those men had a right to kill at least *one* of you. I mean, didn't you kill *all* of them?"

"Of course. We wanted their guns and ponies. No man will give you his gun and pony unless you kill him first."

"But who gave you the right to own all the guns and ponies in the first place? Don't you think other people have the right to keep what's theirs?"

"Certainly, if they are strong enough to keep us from taking it."

"Don't you people respect anything but brute force?"

"We see many things worthy of our respect. We see lightning on the mountaintops, the bright face of the sun as it soars across the sky, the power and the beauty of an eagle as it dives towards its prey."

"But don't you see anything you like in people?"

"I like my family and friends. I think I like *you*. I know I liked Poinsenay. That is why I tried to please his ghost by making those White Eyes pay for killing him."

"I just don't understand you, Eskinya. You've been so gentle with La Señora, her children, and me. I've seen you laugh when the other children teased you, and you treat your ponies like they were fluffy little kittens. Yet, last night with that knife in your hand . . ."

"You should not have looked. If you had stayed back with the old yellow-haired captive and her skinny daughter, you would not have been frightened by our ways. I left you with the women, remember? It was your idea to press forward and join Poinsenay's family as they mourned him."

"I heard his wife screaming and went to comfort her! How was I to know I'd find her chewing on a white man's insides like a dog?"

"What do your women do when one of their men is killed?"

"Well, we don't carry on like wild animals! Oh, I suppose we scream and cry a lot. I suppose, if someone killed her loved ones, a white woman would kill their murderer if she had the chance. But to cut a man to bits like that and listen to him scream for hours . . ."

"You speak of *white* women," the Indian cut in with a puzzled frown. "You are not white. At least, you say you are not white. Have you changed your mind as to what you are?"

"Of course not. I told you I'm a black captive."

"Then what concern is it of yours what a white woman would or would not do if someone killed her husband? You told me your people are held captive by these strangers. I should think you would like it when we killed them."

"Well, I don't. I've never hated anyone bad enough to want to see them dead."

"Then you like to be a captive?"

"I never said that. I only said I didn't hate the way you do." She thought a moment as they rode on. Then she said, "When I was young and didn't know any better, I used to dream of running away and being free. I'd heard of a place called Canada, where it was against the law to hold colored people against their will. I told myself, someday I'd go there and be free. Canada would be just like Africa, and I'd never have to do anything I didn't want to again."

"Why didn't you go there?"

"Because I was afraid. They told us that white men hunted runaways for money and that our masters would whip us if we tried to be free. When I was just a baby, a black man called Nat Turner killed his master and tried to be free. They used to show us pictures of Nat Turner, hanging on a rope, all dead and rotting. They told us that was what happened to people like us if we didn't behave."

Eskinya shrugged. "If I had been born a black White Eyes, I think I would have killed the people who frightened you and taken you to this Canada place. Would you have liked that, Hey-Zabel?"

"I guess I would have. All but the killing. If you had been born on our plantation, I know you would have run away. I'll bet you would have made it, too!"

"Ha! Maybe when we got to this Canada, I would have stolen many ponies and we would have been very rich. What are the ponies like in your Canada?"

"I don't know. I never went there. But if you'd been there . . . Well, never mind. We're just talking foolishly."

Further up the column, Willy Unger felt warm and uncomfortable. The sun was shining, and he closed his eyes to snuggle deeper into the rocking softness that surrounded him. It smelled funny in the wagon bed this morning. He seemed to be sort of sitting up, and the blankets smelled of smoke and maybe cornhusks. Willy opened his eyes again and stared weakly up into a strange face carved from polished rosewood. Willy muttered, "Hey, you ain't my Ma!" and two eyes as black as pools of ink met his with an expression that might have seemed tender to an Indian child. The strange woman holding him said, *"Diit-ash-*

nleidi," and swung her pony as Willy struggled to sit up, demanding, "Where's my ma? I want my ma!"

Ernestine, half dozing on Digoon's pony, heard her son's voice and nearly fell as she sat bolt upright to scream, "Willy. Where are you?"

Nearby on Naiche's mount, Alfrieda yelled, "I see him, Momma! He's awake and that Injun woman's carryin' him back to us!"

There was a moment of confusion as Cho-Ko-Ley rode against the movement of the others to meet the recovered boy's mother. Willy Unger was totally bewildered as he spotted his mother in the swirl, and waved and called. "What happened, Ma? Where did all these Injuns come from?"

Ernestine jumped off the pony as Cho-Ko-Ley lowered the still-weak boy to her with no expression on her broad brown face. Ernestine wrapped her arms around the child she'd given up for lost and began to cry as Willy muttered, "Aw, gee, Ma, what are you blubberin' 'bout?"

By this time Eskinya and Jezebel had ridden up, and the black girl jumped off to run to her mistress, asking, "Is he all right, Mizz Ernestine?"

"His fever's broke at last! My God, I thought we'd lost him!"

"You want me to thank this Injun lady, ma'am?"

"What? What do you mean, Jezebel?"

"This lady here, ma'am. She's Eskinya's ma, and do I say thanks to him in Spanish, he kin tell her what you said in their own lingo."

Ernestine looked up at the impassive brown woman staring down at her and Willy, and stammered, "Oh, of course. I suppose she might have helped with those Indian herbs at that. I suppose it's only proper to say *something* about it to her, don't you think?"

Jezebel said, "Yes'm, I 'spose it is."

IT WAS NEARLY noon by the time Rabbit-Boss cut the trail of the northbound Nadene. He'd led the patrol on a northeast course, rather than directly toward the place the young Digger couple had crossed it the day before. The short cut saved them miles of travel, even as it added to Matt Caldwell's confusion. He'd heard these primitives had strange powers, but he'd never put much faith in the stories before meeting this uncanny Indian tracker.

The desert seemed to be opening out and getting flatter as they let Rabbit-Boss lead them into its dead heart. According to Digger Greenberg, it got worse ahead. It was hard to see how. The clumps of dead or dying vegetation were widely spaced, and the exposed white gravel between the clumps was dry as blackboard chalk. Caldwell swung in his Tuareg saddle for a look back the way they'd come. Here and there a camel had left a faint heart-shaped depression in a soft spot, but most of the surface was firmer than a well-paved gravel roadway back east. Greenberg had called the stuff "caliche" and explained that wind had blown the fine grains from the soil, while mineral salts from below had cemented the remaining larger particles together until it took a good solid blow to break through the crust.

When they found the Apaches' trail, of course, the caliche had been broken and scuffed much more by the harder, smaller hooves of the Indian ponies. Even Caldwell saw the trail when Rabbit-Boss pointed it out to him. How their tracker read the direction of the Indian column, or was able to tell the mark of a burro from that of a horse, was anybody's guess. To everyone but Greenberg and his Indian, they were simply dents in the otherwise featureless surface of skeleton gray. The trail took them due north, as Greenberg had suggested it would. Caldwell pointed to a distant ridge of purple mountains to his right and asked the scout if they had a name.

Greenberg squinted and opined, "Too low to be the Providence Ranges. Most likely they ain't on the map yet."

"Where's the Colorado River from here?"

"Other side of them fer hills. We'uns is in another basin now. Ain't no river worth mention this fur southeast of the Mojave, and that ain't sayin' the Mojave's all that much this late in the summer."

"How far would this Mojave be? I don't remember seeing it on Fremont's map."

"I'd say it's a good hundred miles to water fit fer pigs, and it ain't on Fremont's map 'cause Fremont never mapped the real desert. Him and Kit Carson follered the ridges like sensible folk. Here and there a ridge of high ground cuts across the grain fer some damn reason. Fremont calt them the Transverse Ranges. They start with the Santa Monicas and San Bernardinos over near the ocean, them dwindle out into the Chocolates, Chuckawallas, and sech, till you met up with the Colorado Delta. The delta's flat but well watered, and you kin cross to Yuma and the Gila down thataway."

"Are there no easy routes across it this far north?"

"Nope. You kin mebbe foller the Mojave east from the San Bernardinos till it starts to run salty. Then if you fill your canteens and scoot due northeast to the Eagle Crags, you just might make it without you kill your ponies." He spit and added, " 'Course, iffen you miss the Eagles and ride betwixt them and the Providence Ranges, you wind up in Death Valley and that kin be a bother. Death Valley ain't as bad as where them fool Apache is leadin' us. You got Furnace Creek and a few scattered water holes in Death Valley, but it's one hell of a place to be in summer."

"Jesus, I thought Death Valley was what they called the worst part of this desert!"

"Shoot, them pioneers as named Death Valley never seed the *real* desert! I'll allow some of 'em died up thataway, crossin' in summer durin' the gold rush back in forty-nine, but like I said, there's a little water in Death Valley. Why, shoot, there's even Injuns living there!"

Caldwell rode silently for a time, working on his mental arithmetic. He asked the scout how wide the central basin they were riding into was, and Greenberg answered, "Hard to say. You kin see fer your ownself it don't have a fence about it. I'd allow the really bad part might be fifty, sixty miles across, by a hundred and fifty north and south."

"In other words, at thirty miles or more a day . . ."

"Hold on, it ain't that simple. We'uns ain't jawin' about no billiard table, Lieutenant. Them headin's I jest gave you would be as the crow flies. Only we ain't ridin' no damn crows. Them Injuns and ussen is mounted on critters with *laigs!*"

"I don't see what's so complicated, Digger. These camels can go a week or more without food and water, and we've three or four days' water ration in our canteens. It seems to me we could move into any part of this basin at will."

"Your seemin' has a lot of larnin' to do, then. I tolt you it ain't no billiard game. This low country is nigh dead flat, but nigh ain't exact. Some parts is lower'n others. This heartland of the desert is where all the water runs to, when and if it runs at all."

"All right, so there may be a few shallow lakes or marshes out in the middle."

"A few, my ass! There's hundreds of part-time lakes and brine swamps out ahead of ussen! The big ones ain't so bad. You kin see 'em to go around. Shoot, you come up the Colorado on a steamboat, Lieutenant, you mind how twisty and turny and all mixed up the sand and water was?"

"Certainly, the Lower Colorado is a braided steam bed."

"Well, the country we'uns is headed into like a pack of fools is a braided swamp. A salty, pi'zen, underground swamp. You follow me?"

"I'm not sure I do. I don't see how a salt marsh or any other can be buried under the earth. I mean, if it's full of earth, it's hardly a swamp, is it?"

"Well, wait til you break through the caliche and drown your fool self in salty quicksand, then. You see, that sun-ball up there bakes the surface dry as bones, but under the salt flats and sand dunes up ahead, a hell of a mess of winter rainwater jest sits and waits fer some damn fool to come along and pickle his fool self in spite of good advice."

"In other words, we'll have to watch our step from here on out."

"The best way to watch it would be to turn around afore it's too late."

Two hundred yards ahead, a flock of buzzards suddenly rose against the northern sky, as Rabbit-Boss, on point, disturbed them to approach a cluster of dark forms stretched out among the greasewood clumps. The others rode forward, but the Indian waved them off, shouting, "Your Spirit Horses will buck you off if you try to bring them closer!"

Caldwell raised his right hand to halt the patrol, then knelt his camel as Trooper Dorfler did the same for his and Greenberg's. The lieutenant slid out of the saddle and walked stiffly over to join the Indian. Rabbit-Boss pointed at one of the cadavers near his feet and said quietly, "This one was alive when they opened him up to build the fire in his belly. I think he was a white man. Some of the others were."

Matt Caldwell gagged in horror as he realized the mangled mess of charred and bloody flesh had once been a human being. Digger Greenberg joined him, spit, and said, "Them buzzards done some of the damage, I'll allow, but them old boys was purely worked on by the squaws a mite. I'd say these hombres musta kilt themselves an Injun or two afore they went under."

Caldwell knew he was going to throw up in front of his men, but he couldn't help it. He staggered off to one side, bent over, and let it come up. Behind him, another man retched, and managed to gag, "My God! Them Injuns peeled this one's head like an orange!"

The ground beneath him seemed to sway as Caldwell heard Greenberg opine, "He musta been a Mexican. Apache don't scalp much, 'lessen they catch a Mexican. Them jaspers has long memories, and they like to pay the governor of Sonora back when they gits the chance."

"I'm going to fall down," Caldwell marveled dully. Then someone steadied him, and the voice of High Jolly soothed, "It is hard the first few times, Effendi. The trick is not to look too closely, and not to picture them as they might have looked in life."

Caldwell straightened up, shook off the helping hand of the Muslim, and growled, "When did you ever fight Indians before?"

"In another desert, Effendi, and they were called Bedouin. The habits of the desert dweller are everywhere the same, though Allah be more merciful."

Recovering himself, Caldwell smiled weakly at High Jolly and said, "I'm sorry I snapped at you. You must think I acted like a fool."

"Does Allah create a man a fool because he gives him a compassionate heart? Truly, Effendi, the first time I found a man the Bedouin had been toying with, I did more than vomit. By my very God, I screamed and wept like a woman. Since then, I have learned to steel myself, but I feel no shame for my tears that first time. *Inshallah,* if more men wept at the sight of blood, there would be much less spilled in this imperfect world!"

Caldwell wiped a hand across his mouth. "I'm not supposed to break down like that. I'm a soldier."

"I know, Effendi. The rules are the same in every army. The next time you will not retch, and if you are anything like the officers in the Turkish army, there will come a time, though Allah must have His own good reasons, when you will be able to do the same thing to an enemy. In my old country, when the Turks caught a Bedouin raider, they started by castrating him and ended it with his head on a pole."

Caldwell grimaced and said, "Thanks for your words of cheer. I'll be all right, I think."

He walked back to where Rabbit-Boss was probing in a bush with his stick. The Indian straightened up as he approached, and said, "There were twelve of your people killed, if you count two Mexicans as your people. The Snakes took fifteen horses and at least twelve guns along with such food and water as these people had."

"What were you looking at in that clump of brush?"

"Glass. Brown glass. Some whiskey bottles were broken here. Some of them had never been opened. I am trying to read what this might mean."

Caldwell shrugged. "What does it matter? Some supplies probably caught a few bullets in the fighting. Did the Apache scatter as usual after they finished here?"

"Yes, but not far. They only left a few false trails, and bodies are still here. I think Diablito does not know we trail him. Or he knows and does not care. There were as many here as you have riding with you. They killed one Snake before they were beaten."

"They got one Apache? How can you tell?"

Rabbit-Boss pointed to the west with his chin, "A body is buried over that way. They thought to hide the signs of digging, but my people are skilled at digging and I found the secret grave as soon as I looked for it. The Snakes you call Apache always bury their dead to the west. The dead man is sitting there now, gazing westward under the gravel."

"My God, did you dig him up? We've only been here a few minutes!"

Rabbit-Boss frowned. The Blue Sleeves made so many jokes, and it was hard to tell when they were serious or simply stupid. He said, "I did not open the grave," and turned away.

Caldwell turned and shouted, "Corporal Muller, two-man detail to see what this Indian's talking about. He says there's a dead Apache buried over there. Dig the bastard up and see if he's right."

Rabbit-Boss knew the Blue Sleeves would never find the spot. So he sauntered over to stand by until they'd satisfied themselves. What was the matter with them? Didn't they know Snakes always buried their dead in a sitting position facing west? Did they think the Snakes had taken time to bury anyone else? Truly, these Blue Sleeves wasted much talk and motion on the obvious. It was no wonder they needed so much food and water.

Muller had two troopers break out entrenching tools and sent them over to the Indian. Then he asked Caldwell, "What about these others, sir? Do you want a burial detail?"

Caldwell nodded, and when Greenberg started to mutter under his breath about wasted effort, he said, "One mass grave, Corporal Muller. Make sure you bury all the pieces."

"What about their clothes and boots and such, sir? Them Injuns sorta scattered things all about before they rode off."

"Put it all in the same hole and I'll read a few words over the remains. Let's get cracking, Corporal. We haven't got all day."

"Yes, sir, I guess you aim to catch them rascals and pay 'em back good, don't you, sir?"

Matt Caldwell's eyes were dry and hard as he nodded. "That's about the size of it. Be ready to move out in half an hour. I don't care if the bastards know we're here or not!"

THE FIRST PONY died that afternoon. Eskinya cut the throat of Hummingbird-Dancer when he saw his lame animal could go no farther. The women gathered round when he announced his decision, and every precious drop of blood was caught in tightly woven baskets. Some was drunk at once, for the people were thirsty and there was no cactus on the playa to quench their thirst. The rest would dry to blood sausage, along with the meat they stripped from the choice parts of the dead pony. Most of the meat was left, for there was no time to butcher properly, and they knew the other ponies would start dying unless they came to sweet water in the next few days. The Nadene people could last four days without fresh water, if there was any moisture at all in the food they carried with them, but while a burro may last nearly as long as a man without a drink, ponies could not. The White Eyes watered their big mounts every day. Indian ponies could manage if they drank their fill every other day. After that, they began to die. It was strange how such a large, strong animal could be weaker than a Nadene child when it came to its stomach. With ponies half as tough as their riders, there would be no place the Nadene could not go. Horseflesh was the weak link in Kaya-Tenay's chain of conquests. With the right ponies, he was sure he'd be able to go anywhere he wanted, take anything he wanted, and kill as many enemies as lay in wait around the moving domain of his people.

The captives refused to drink the blood of Hummingbird-Dancer when it was offered to them. Eskinya tried to understand Jezebel's reluctance as she joined the Unger family in expressions of disgust. He asked her, "Do your people not eat meat?" and when she tried to explain the difference between horseflesh, venison, and pork, he found her words confusing. From what she told him, the White Eyes ate *fish,* which no Nadene in his hungriest moment would dream of doing. Yet she refused even to taste the blood of a fine pony like Hummingbird-Dancer. Eskinya was about to tell her the jerked meat she and the others had been eating was an assortment of venison, bighorn, burro, and pony. Then he considered his pretty captive's apparent lack of humor and decided to wait. A wise man tames a skittish pony with a gentle hand and soothing words.

The butchering took little time, but everyone not directly involved took advantage of the short break to rest their mounts and ease their cramped legs. Ernestine Unger and Alfrieda walked some distance out across the sun-baked lake bottom unguarded and, apparently, ignored. This was only apparently, however. Digoon and Naiche were too considerate to follow a woman closely when she had to relieve herself, but Eskinya had told them he did not think either of his friends would be careless enough to let one of his prisoners escape, and though they appeared to ignore the two distant dots squatting on the lake bed, they never lost track of them for an instant.

Willy Unger, still weak from his close brush with death, had managed to strike up an inarticulate understanding with the Indian children around him. When one of the Nadene boys slapped Willy lightly as an experiment, Willy punched him on the cheek. Neither was hurt, but since Indian children didn't hit with fists, the new boy's blow had made them decide it might be better to teach Willy to play Kah. This was a Nadene game similar to "Button, button, who's got the button?" and one could win or lose without tears or bruises. Willy wasn't as good at Kah as he might have been at schoolboy fisticuffs, so none of his new acquaintances felt any need to even the odds with a weapon. There wasn't a boy in the band who could have beaten Willy in a fist-fight—or would have been unable to kill him easily. Eight-year-old Nadene boys had been receiving instructions in knife fighting, lance-thrusting, riding, roping, and the bow and arrow since they were old enough to talk. If Willy felt a certain superiority in rough-housing about the camp with the other boys, it was because Nadene were unfamiliar with how one handles himself in a *friendly* tussle.

Cho-Ko-Ley watched from a distance in silent approval. The child she'd saved was strong for his age, despite his recent illness. His bones were big, and she knew he would grow to be a giant of a man. The yellow-haired one seemed attached to him, too, but if she were offered her freedom and many ponies, she would doubtless give him up. The husky, long-limbed boy would make a fine Nadene, once they taught him the Way of the People.

She would have to speak of this with Kaya-Tenay, but not now. Her husband had been sipping at the American tiswin in the thick brown glass bottles, and when Kaya-Tenay was drinking tiswin, it was not a good idea to approach him.

Eskinya knew it was a bad time to talk to his father, too. Kaya-Tenay sat his pony a little distance from the others, as he waited for them to finish with the butchering, or perhaps just waited for some sign as to what he should do next. He should have been resting the pony during the short break in their weary march across the playa, but there are times a man had difficulty getting back upon his pony, and the brown tequila of the White Eyes was stronger than the tiswin he was used to.

As the people finished with their chores and started getting ready to move out again, Eskinya walked over to where his father sat his pony and said, "I think this playa is bad for our animals. The salts are making their hoofs sore."

Kaya-Tenay stared bleary-eyed at his son and mumbled, "What are you doing down there? Why are you not mounted like a Husband? Some of my people are mounted and others are on foot. It is all very confusing."

"We have stopped to butcher one of my ponies. His leg went bad and the salt and dust of this place finished him. I think, if we keep to these dry playas, the other animals will go lame, too."

"We will be across this bad country soon. Get back on your pony and follow me. By nightfall, we shall have crossed this playa."

"Hear me, my father, I mean you no insult, but I think you may be wrong. I have been watching the hills spread out as we rode north, and now we are as ants in a big, shallow bowl. I fear you lead us ever downward to the center of this bowl. I think it would be better if we turned to the east."

Kaya-Tenay blinked owlishly. "Why should we turn east? I don't know what you're talking about."

"Mountains are to be seen over that way. We have lost sight of the hills to our west, and there are none to the north. I think the eastern mountains must be high, and that means they must be well watered."

"I shall find plenty of water to the *north*."

"Forgive me, but I do not think so. There may be bad water that way. We are too far from any hills for the water to be fit to drink. This land is flat. There are no washes to take cover in, and our women cannot cook our food when it gets dark. It will get cold out here when the sun goes down, and we are caught in the open, exposed to every wind and to any passing eye. If we started now for those distant hills . . ."

"Your open mouth is fit only for attracting flies!" cut in Kaya-Tenay with an angry wave of his arm that nearly made him fall from his not-too-steady seat atop his pony. He recovered his balance, and some of his dignity, to add in a more reasonable tone, "I have an understanding with the voices. If we keep going the way they have chosen, we shall come at last to the green lands of our ancestors. Do not the legends tell of such a place in the long before?"

"My father, the legends say our people came up from a lower world through dangerous caves to the surface of this world."

"Yes, and the land here keeps sloping ever downward to the north! We only have to find the big cave leading down into the one-time home of our people and . . . You shall see, my son. I know what I am trying to say, but the words do not form on my tongue!"

"Father, I think I understand what you are searching for, but no such land exists."

"What's this you say? Do you say the legends are not true?"

"I think, if they are true, much meaning has been lost in the many tellings. I think the old ones remember other lands from before the Beginning. I think, if these other lands had been so good, our legends would not call them dark and cold, nor rejoice in our escape out into the sunlight."

Kaya-Tenay shook his head and tears ran down his bronzed cheeks as he insisted, "It was a *good* place. Our people had no enemies before they came up through the caves to fight the bears, the Utes, the Pueblos, and now the White Eyes! The voices say, if we keep going north, we shall come to a land no enemies know about. We shall come to a land where only Nadene live, in happiness with fat ponies and much game. I have heard the voices and I believe them."

"Has my father spoken?"

"I have spoken. We go *north*. We go north now!"

Eskinya shrugged and walked back to where he'd left Jezebel and his pony in the care of Naiche. Jezebel and Alfrieda Unger were on foot and arguing about something in their own language. The black girl seemed flushed and angry, and the younger captive had obviously been teasing her. Eskinya nodded at Naiche and vaulted up on the saddle blanket before he

146

turned to look down at Jezebel and ask in Spanish,
"Do you wish to ride on another pony? We have many
now if you would like me to give you one."

Jezebel hesitated. Then she held up a hand and said,
"I'd feel safer up there with you. I don't know much
about horses."

Eskinya nodded, took her wrist, and pulled her easily from the ground as Alfrieda jeered, "Jezebel! Sweet
on her old Injun boyfriend, like I just said!"

Eskinya frowned, not sure of the joke but aware of
the mockery in the young girl's tone. He asked Jezebel,
"Is that young White Eyes making fun of me?" and
Jezebel said, "No, she's making fun of me. She seems
to think I like you."

"Oh? Is it such a joke for you and me to be friends?"

"It is to her, I suppose."

MATT CALDWELL FELT better about things once he'd
led his patrol out on the dead flat expanse of the open
playa. Mounted tactics were taught as if the world were
a featureless table top, and for the first time since he'd
ridden out into this harsh and dangerous country, he
knew, or thought he knew, what he was doing.

Outriders were posted just outside of rifle range on
either flank. The others rode dressed in echelon in a
slanting line to Caldwell's left and rear, with Corporal
Muller bringing up the rear. The naked Rabbit-Boss,
on point, was not in the book. Neither was Digger
Greenberg, being led by Trooper Dorfler off to
Caldwell's right. But he'd been taught to be flexible,
and they weren't exactly advancing to make contact
with the usual enemy skirmish line.

Another thing that pleased the officer was the pony tracks. For the first time since leaving the fort, Caldwell was able to read signs in the dusty surface instead of counting on his civilian scout and the Indian. The hoofprints leading due north were clear and crisp in the ocher surface of the old lake bed, and Caldwell was able to tell those of the shod mounts taken from Diablito's white victims from those of his Apache ponies or burros. The tracks seemed fresh, and Caldwell judged there were at least six dozen separate sets of them. He peered at the heat-hazed horizon for any sign of his quarry and reflected, as he failed to spot so much as a sign of dust, that there was simply no way the Apache could ambush them out here. His outriders were clearly visible on either side, albeit safely out a mile. Diablito would simply have to stand and fight when the patrol caught up with him. They would catch up, Caldwell knew.

Rabbit-Boss set a slower pace than a trotting pony was capable of, but as Greenberg had pointed out, the tireless Digger could jog mile after mile without a break, whereas no pony could carry a load in this heat without being rested every hour or so. The Diggers ran down rabbit and antelope in open desert, according to the scout. It was becoming clear, watching Rabbit-Boss, why they preferred to hunt out here on foot. They weren't too stupid to see the advantages of ponies. They'd learned from experience that no animal is as tough and determined a desert runner as a human being in good shape. A hundred species could run faster than a man, for a time, but unless the animal found a way to cover its tracks, a stubborn human hunter would sooner or later run it into the ground. To Rabbit-Boss, an Apache pony was simply another form of prey he'd follow, at that mile-eating lope of his, until he'd simply worn it down. The human prey riding the ponies was another matter, but the Apache were not the Digger's concern. His job would be done when the two sides were within shooting range of one another.

Caldwell swung his mount closer to that of High Jolly just to his left and said. "At the rate we're moving, we must be gaining on them, don't you think?"

High Jolly nodded. "No horse can outdistance El Jamal in country such as this." Then the Muslim swung in his saddle to stare back at the faint heart-shaped depressions their own mounts were leaving on the sun-baked surface. Caldwell caught the look of concern in High Jolly's eyes and asked, "What's the matter? You don't look too happy. Are you worried about those Apache up ahead?"

High Jolly shook his head. "Though Ahriman is their brother and the scorpion their mother, I believe this time those red Infidels have overreached themselves. Observe, Effendi, how even our own tracks are visible now as we progress ever deeper into this chott!"

"Chott?" frowned Caldwell.

"Ah, yes, in this desert you call it a playa, but in any desert it is treacherous. The surface that we ride across is clay baked, though Allah be more merciful, by a cruel relentless sun."

"That's easy enough to see. What's the problem?"

"A sharp knife would scratch it, *Inshallah,* but the foot of a mere man should not be able to dent it, and El Jamal treads more softly than any human foot."

"All right, the clay is not as hard as it looks."

"Clay is clay, Effendi Lieutenant. It is hard when dry, and soft when . . . wet!"

"Oh, come on, it hasn't rained out here in years. That hardpan's dry as a bone. Watch Rabbit-Boss out there. See the dust he's stirring up as he scuffs across it?"

"I did not say the clay is wet on its *surface,* Effendi. You must understand something about these low places in the desert. They are the last refuge of any water there may be. Truly, any rain that Allah may provide in this desolate valley must sink into the earth

149

or blow away again on the desert wind. Clay is a thirsty soil. If it can possibly hold water, it does so. I think a few inches down, the lake bed must be moist. To take the footprint of El Jamal, it must be moist indeed."

Before he could answer, Caldwell saw Rabbit-Boss out in front stop dead in his tracks and drop to one knee. Caldwell reined in and held up his free hand to halt the column. He walked Fatima slowly forward as he watched the Indian probing the surface ahead of him with his digging stick. Rabbit-Boss stood up, pointed the stick to the east, and said, "Better we go that way."

Greenberg joined Caldwell as he asked the Indian. "What about you talking about? Those Apache tracks lead due north! What's over there to the east?"

"Mountains," said Rabbit-Boss, apparently not caring to elaborate.

Greenberg said, "No way they's gonna make it across this big playa. If there's water under the crust this close to the edges, the middle has to be worse."

Caldwell stared down at the apparently solid surface. "All right, why does Rabbit-Boss think they'll swing east? Wouldn't west do just as well?"

"Sure, if all they aimed at was dry ground. Trouble with the desert to the west is it's too danged dry, where it ain't wet. Betwixt here and the Mojave Draw, there's miles of salt marsh, alkali flats, and sech."

"What if they made their way through this inland delta to the north and east, Digger?"

"Shoot, they'd be home free with clear water all the way to the San Bernardinos." Then he spit and added, "Only, they ain't about to make it. You see where them pony hooves has cut through the crust in spots? Them ponies need a wade through sweet water and a walk through dry, clean sand to scour the alkali outten their frogs afore they all wind up lame."

Greenberg pointed at one set of tracks. "That pony's done fer already. They've took off its load and it's still limpin' on three laigs. They'll likely butcher it afore it goes another thirty miles."

Caldwell sat quietly and stared to the north from the vantage point of Fatima's hump. He said, "You may be right, but I've got a bird in the hand here. If we leave the trail on your Indian's opinion that they'll swing toward those Providence Ranges to the east . . ."

"Rabbit-Boss don't have opinions!" Greenberg cut in. "He's thinkin' one jump ahead of them Apache, and if they has sense to pour piss outten their boots, they'll be makin' fer the Providence right about now!"

"I can see that, Digger, but what if they don't have sense? Diablito doesn't know this country as well as Rabbit-Boss. What if he just keeps bulling ahead the way he's going?"

Greenberg spit. "He winds up daid, as any fool kin see. It ain't like them Apache has a choice, goddamn it! Their ponies is leaving tracks already, an' we ain't a fifth of the way to the center of this durned lake. While we'uns sit here jawin' 'bout it, them Injuns is either mired to their durned knees in washin' soda or half ways to the mountains yonder!"

Caldwell turned to High Jolly and asked, "What do you say, drover?"

The Muslim looked surprised and grinned. "By the Beard Of the Prophet, I will follow you anywhere, Effendi but, though Allah be more merciful, our mounts must have solid ground to walk upon."

"You don't think we can push on out to where we see the Indians have been bogging down and then decide which way to go?"

"Forgive these poor beasts, Effendi, but they are not as willing as horses to let themselves be driven into danger. From the look of the surface and the attitude of our mounts, I would say we could perhaps persuade them to go on a few more miles. Long before the first sign of a horseman in distress, however, El Jamal will have balked. These are timid creatures of the desert,

Effendi, and they sense its treachery long before a man or horse."

Caldwell shrugged. "I guess I'm outvoted. We'll head for those ranges to the east and see if we can cut them off, but I hope we know what we're doing."

The officer nodded to Rabbit-Boss, and as the Indian started jogging northeast, Caldwell gave the hand signal for echelon-right. He saw the outrider to his east rein in and stare across the flat at them for a few moments before getting the new bearing, waving, and moving into the new position on the right flank. To the west, where he was now far to the rear of the column, Trooper Csonka raced his camel to take up his new position as left flank outrider. Caldwell glanced back once or twice to make sure Csonka understood, and then ignored him, as did everyone else while they dressed their line to advance in echelon on the Providence Range. Nobody thought about the fact that Trooper Csonka had no idea why they'd changed course. He was moving fast to the north to fall in again on their flank. What could happen to an armed man in the middle of a wide-open playa?

What happened was that Csonka's camel balked, nearly throwing the former Czarist cavalry officer over its neck as it felt the brittle crust give just a fraction of an inch under its soft front pads.

Csonka cursed as the cruciform pommel of the saddle dug into his belly, and he fought to recover his balance. The Pole was a good rider and considerate of his mount. He stared down to see what had spooked his camel and, seeing nothing, shouted, "*Hike! Hike!* What's the matter with you, *kapusta leniwaya?*"

The patrol was moving away, and Csonka began to scream and curse in a mixture of English, Polish, and Arabic to no avail. The camel simply refused to budge.

"*Swinia brudny!*" The angry trooper shouted, leaping to the ground with the rein in one hand and his camel goad in the other. Csonka's intention had been to lead the unruly beast over, around, or through whatever invisible demons seemed to be freezing it in its tracks. He was quite surprised when he found himself standing knee-deep in something warm and wet in the middle of an apparently endless desert!

The sun-baked crust, once broken, began to give all around as the frightened camel backed away, moaning and burbling its way to firmer footing. Fortunately for Csonka, the trooper had the presence of mind to hang on tightly to the rein. The mixture of clay, water, borax and lye sucked Csonka's boots off and slowly started to digest them as the camel pulled him out of the ever-widening maw of hungry mud. By the time the embarrassed trooper was clear and stamping around on the harder surface his mount had deposited him on, the others had noted his difficulty and stopped. Caldwell signaled Muller to keep his men dressed in position as he, High-Jolly, Greenberg, and Rabbit-Boss headed back to Csonka's aid.

Rabbit-Boss reached Csonka first. Without ceremony, the Indian knocked the Pole down and proceeded to tear his pants off. Csonka roared, "Have you gone crazy?" and tried to struggle free. Then Digger Greenberg called, "Get outten them duds and do it now! That's nigh to pure lye water you been wallerin' about in like a damn fool hog!"

Caldwell, understanding better than his confused trooper, shouted, "Strip, Csonka! That's an order!"

Csonka offered no resistance as the Indian finished pulling off his clothes, but he got to his feet and stared open-mouthed at Rabbit-Boss as the Indian held the hands he'd touched the wet uniform with out in front of himself and calmly urinated into his cupped palms.

Digger Greenberg said, "Piss all over the sojer, Rabbit-Boss." But as the naked Csonka cowered away in open-mouthed confusion, Rabbit-Boss said, "Not enough in me to help. Maybe Spirit Horses piss on him good before him die."

The Muslim shook his head. "El Jamal does not do such a thing on command. He keeps his water in his belly, where it will do him the most good. I have a small bottle of vinegar among my stores, if the Effendi Lieutenant thinks we can spare water."

Caldwell stared down at the embarrassed Csonka, who aside from his nakedness seemed as good as ever, Caldwell knew, however, about chemical burns. He asked, "How much water do you think you'll need to wash that lye away before it does permanent damage, High Jolly?"

The Muslim shrugged. "If the waters he fell into are half as strong as those I know in another desert, much damage has been done already. If I use all my vinegar and most of your water, *Inshallah,* we may save his life."

Csonka scratched at his groin, winced, and held his fingers up to the light. Then he straightened to attention, stared soberly up at his officer, and asked, "Permission to shoot myself, sir? I seem to be losing all my skin from the waist down and, please, sir, it *hurts!"*

THE SUN WAS setting and the shadows of the People were long upon the cracked surface when Eskinya did a very rude thing. He heeled his pony up beside that of Kenya-Tenay, leaned forward, and grabbed the older man's bridle. The two mounts reared in confusion as Kaya-Tenay struck wildly at his son, hitting the black captive girl with the flat of his bow instead. Jezebel screamed more in fright than pain, and the younger Indian grabbed the bow from his father, snapping, "I do not wish to hurt you, but you will not hit my woman again and live!"

Surprised as much by the words as the insulting behavior of his oldest son, Kaya-Tenay shook his head to clear it and muttered, "I think you must have had more tiswin than myself, Eskinya! You are so drunk your words fly in every direction like rising quail."

"My father, you must listen to me. The ponies keep breaking through this frail crust you've led us out on. The mud below is eating hair and hooves from more than seven animals, and I think we'll have to kill them, even if we get them out of here!"

"Bah! Your voice is the voice of a woman. Has that black White-Eyed girl been teaching you to speak, Eskinya?"

"I did not stop your pony to talk about our captives, my father. I stopped you because you are leading us to certain destruction!"

"I lead you to the safe green hunting grounds of long ago. Let go my bridle. I know how to thread my way between the soft spots we seem to be encountering. This is not the first bad country I have crossed, you know."

"Listen to me, my father, it is getting dark and the ankles of your pony are raw. You have had too much tiswin and don't know what you are doing. I think you should at least make camp here for the night. In the morning . . ."

"Let go of my bridle. I have spoken," Kaya-Tenay insisted, slapping wildly with his open palm and catching Jezebel across one upflung arm as she ducked her head against Eskinya's broad shoulders. The younger Nadene let go his father's bridle and danced his pony out of the old man's reach. In Spanish he soothed, "That will never happen again, Hey-Zabel," and the girl replied, "I'm all right, but what was that all about?"

"My father is drunk. Unless he comes to his senses in time, his people are doomed. Our ponies cannot live in this country, and what is a man without a pony?"

Before Jezebel could answer, Eskinya's mother, Cho-Ko-Ley rode up beside them and asked in Nadene, "What were you and your father fighting about? If he wants this woman, you should give her to him. I know you like her, but she is a captive. She has no rights of refusal unless one of the Real Women has adopted her into one of the clans."

Eskinya shook his head. "That is not what we were fighting about, my mother. The old fool is drunk and he keeps riding his pony through the soft spots. The pony is already growing lame and . . ."

"How dare you speak that way about your father in front of this black White Eyes?" Cho-Ko-Ley cut in savagely.

Eskinya said, "The girl does not know our tongue, and besides, I have to speak out against his madness before it's too late. The others are afraid of Kaya-Tenay when he has been drinking, but I am not. I am more afraid of losing all our ponies that I am of his temper, or the spirits he talks to when he's been at the tiswin."

Cho-Ko-Ley gasped and raised her hand to strike. Then she turned her face away. "You never knew him when he was younger and our people were feared from the Gila to the Yaqui. If you no longer have respect for your father, I think you should go away. There is no room in my heart for such a wicked son."

Eskinya winced as if she'd struck him, and they both knew he could put the matter to rights by simply giving in. But Eskinya sat his horse in silence until his mother started to move on. Then he said, "Hear me, my mother. I think you should let him ride on alone if his mind no longer serves him."

Cho-Ko-Ley didn't answer. Eskinya hadn't expected her to. He and Jezebel sat there, watching the others file past, until Digoon and Naiche reined in with the other captives. Naiche asked, "Why have you stopped here?" and Eskinya replied simply, "I am going off with my prisoners and my ponies. Do you want to come with me?"

Naiche hesitated. Then he said, "Kaya-Tenay is drunk, but he is still my friend."

He waved at the Unger family, each member mounted on its own pony, now, and added, "My woman and I will go where Kaya-Tenay leads us. I don't think the captives will try to escape, but if they do, you have nobody to blame but yourself."

The captives, of course, were unaware of the meaning of this conversation. They watched silently as the Indians argued. Once, Alfrieda asked Jezebel to translate, but the black girl answered, "Just hush and let me listen, Mizz Frieda. I don't mind but ever' third or fourth Injun word, and they seem to be talkin' 'bout us!"

In fact, the disposal of the captives was the least of Eskinya's worries. The fact that they were his was not in dispute. He'd made his move and it was too late to change his mind. Eskinya was leaving the band of Kaya-Tenay. That much was certain. The question was only whether he would leave it alone.

Digoon watched as Naiche rode after the older chief. He pretended a great lack of concern as he said softly to Eskinya, "You will need help in keeping these captives together. I think I'd better go with you."

It was a beginning. Digoon was only a child, and Mexican-born to boot, but he was joined by Taza and the older, tested Ki-E-Ta.

Ki-E-Ta said, "Let me get my two wives and my ponies and we will leave this place." But Eskinya shook his head and said, "We shall wait here until the others have had time to think. My father led these people a long way for a long time. It is too soon for me to expect them to leave his side."

Ki-E-Ta said, "He leads them badly when he listens to the voices in his bottles, but once he was a mighty Husband. I think many of them hope he will recover his senses before he leads them to disaster. If I were you, I would speak out more loudly against Kaya-Tenay. Your words are too soft for a man who would lead his own band."

"You are not me, Ki-E-Ta. Nor am I Kaya-Tenay. The moon will be fat tonight. When it rises above the grass-clad hills to the east, I intend to ride into its rays. Those who wish may ride with me. Those who do not may follow Kaya-Tenay. I have spoken."

He meant, of course, that he was through talking about it in Nadene. Half turning to the girl on the saddle pad behind him, Eskinya spoke in Spanish. "Listen to me. I want you to tell your friends that I am taking them away from here with only a few friends to guard them."

Jezebel started to translate, but the Indian cut in. "I have not finished speaking. You must learn our ways if you intend to follow them. Now, I want you to tell the old yellow-haired woman and her children that I intend to let them go. The boy looks strong and might in time be of use to our nation. But he is still very young and the women are no use to me at all. The mother is too old and scrawny. The daughter will not be old enough for a man to want for at least two years. I know the Blue Sleeves will be out looking for all of you. So I am going to take them to a safe place and release them for the Blue Sleeves to find. I think if the Blue Sleeves recover this family, they may lost interest in following my father's pony tracks."

Jezebel asked, "What do you mean, your father's pony tracks?"

"You interrupt again! You are very beautiful, but you talk too much, even for a woman. When my friends and I ride off with captives and ponies, my father will be very angry. So angry he will want to fight with me. I think we will get away, but Kaya-Tenay will come after us, leading his people out of this death trap. Now do you understand?"

Jezebel laughed and, mixing English with Spanish,

said, "Do Jesus, if you ain't a regular B'rer Rabbit!"

Eskinya frowned and said, "I did not understand that."

In a gentler tone, Jezebel explained, "It's a story my people tell of a very clever rabbit, or maybe a wise black boy. This rabbit, or black boy, or whatever, got people to do what he wanted by asking them to do just the opposite. You don't want to ride off and start your own tribe. You're trying to save the tribe you have by tricking them into chasing you out of this desert! You're trying to make your father so mad at you he'll forget his visions about some Indian fairy land he found in a bottle. You're hoping he'll be so intent on scalping you that he'll drop those bottles and come after you with blood in his eye!"

"I don't think my father would scalp me, but if I can make him remember the man he was, it would not be a bad way to die."

Jezebel felt an odd pang as she gasped, "You don't intend to *die* to save your people, do you, Eskinya?"

The Indian shrugged. "All men die sooner or later. At worst, it can only happen a little sooner. It helps to remember this when a man is forced to make a choice, but if I can keep my father from killing me, I shall take you into the White Mountains with me until my father decides he no longer hates us. My father's mother was a Chiricahua Nadene, and my kinsman Cochise will take us in until everyone's blood has had time to cool. I think you will like it in the White Mountains, Hey-Zabel."

The black captive asked quietly, "What if I don't want to come? Would you take me there against my will?"

Eskinya started to nod, for the captive's question was ridiculous. Then he reconsidered and thought for a time before he answered, "I don't know, I shall have to think about that."

THE SAME SETTING sun was painting the desert rose
and purple a day's journey to the southeast as Rabbit-
Boss jogged on ahead of the camels. The lye-burned
Csonka had been sent toward Fort Havasu in the care
of Trooper Dorfler with orders not to stop before they
got there. Most of their drinking water had been used,
or according to Greenberg, wasted, in washing the
chemical salts from Csonka's second-degree burns.
Smeared with bacon grease and covered with Caldwell's spare clean underwear and a shirt donated by
Muller, Trooper Csonka was going to make it, though
his legs would be scarred for life, or at least until the
Battle of Gettysburg, a few years into the future, where
a Rebel bullet would be waiting with the unlikely
name of Taddeusz Csonka written on it.

The leading of Greenberg's camel had been turned
over to High Jolly, after the Muslim turned down the
chance to ride south with Dorfler and the injured
Csonka. Greenberg had opined High Jolly was a fool,
but Caldwell noticed the sardonic scout himself
seemed willing to play this hand out to its end, whatever that end might be.

The officer was growing accustomed to the unfamiliar gait of Fatima, and while she smelled worse
than any pig and bubbled like a teapot under him,
he had to admit they'd never have made it riding
Army Issue horses, or even mules. From time to time
he caught a sudden glimpse of his own elongated
shadow to the east, and had to laugh at the ridiculous
silhouette the sunset painted on the flat baked clay.
The camel really did look like a horse designed by a

committee. A committee of schoolmarms, at that. He could see why Jefferson Davis's enemies in Congress had hooted at his purchase of nearly a hundred of these funny-looking beasts to send against the Indian nations, but to give the devil his due, the crazy-sounding idea seemed to be working. The camel *was* adapted to the Great American Desert and, given a fair trial by American soldiers willing to learn something new, should form a vital force in the taming of these new lands seized from Mexico in the war.

The sun was setting over Caldwell's left shoulder, but its rays reached across the playa country to etch the distant mountains pink against the purple eastern sky. Caldwell asked Greenberg, "Is that snow over there on those hills?"

The scout shook his head. "Not this time of the year. Must be cloud banners burnin' offen them peaks. The Providence is too high to call hills. It's more like an island of fair-sized ridges out in the middle of no-wheres. Got more desert on the fer side afore you gits to the Colorado, but it's high desert. Not nigh as dry as where we is right now. Do them Apache make it past the Providence, ain't no way in hell we're about to catch 'em."

"I thought we were trying to head them off."

"That's what Rabbit-Boss thinks we oughta do. Iffen it was up to my ownself, we'd be runnin' fer our skins. You got eleven men here, countin' me and that fool Injun. You really reckon to whup thirty or forty Apache with ten guns and that diggin' stick of Rabbit-Boss?"

"It's more like, let's see . . . twenty-eight guns. You and High Jolly have a rifle and pistol each. Muller, his men, and me carry two dragoon pistols and a carbine, so . . ."

"Them carbines don't count fer shit!" Greenberg cut in. "Them muzzle-loaders is only good fer one shot in a fire fight and them Apache bows kin shoot as fer, and a damn sight faster, than them six-guns of your'n.

Sayin' all eleven of us gits off one good rifle shot as they charge, which is too much to hope fer, that still leaves us facing twenty or thirty howlin' mad Apache at point-blank pistol range." He spit and added morosely, "You purely do like long odds, don't you, Lieutenant?"

Matt Caldwell rode a time in silence. The he said, "I thought Apache skulked about, avoiding a stand-up fight in the open."

"Well, sure they does. No man in his right mind cottons to gittin' kilt iffen he kin help it. But look at this country around us, damn it! There ain't no way Diablito's gonna figure on sneakin' up on us out here in all this nothin' much! When we meet up with that old boy, it's gonna be Comanche style. Out in the open and man to man. What do them sojer books of your'n have to say 'bout takin' on a force four times your size in a free-style, no-quarters, kickin'-and-gougin', no-foolin'-around fight?"

"The book says I'm not supposed to do it."

"Well, fer once, your book makes more sense than you do. I'll allow we'd stand a chance dug in ahint some rocks, or even creosote bush fer a mite of cover. Do we reach the Providence well ahead of them Apache rascals and hole up next to water, you got an outside chance of bringin' it off. Them peaks yonder ain't nigh as close as they might look to you, though. Do you aim to beat Diablito to a half-ass chance to make a stand, we'd best pile that fool Injun up here on this critter with me and git crackin'."

"Will Rabbit-Boss ride with you? He seems to be afraid of the camels."

Greenberg spit. "He'll do what I tell him, iffen it makes sense to him. We got us a moon-ball risin' in a mite, and there's no sense him lookin' fer sign on foot out there ahead. A mounted man kin see a quarter mile in moonlight across this dead-flat playa. You want me to take the point?"

Caldwell nodded. "You'd better." Then he called

to High Jolly, "Move Mister Greenberg's mount out
ahead of us, drover."

But Greenberg said, "Keep the fool A-rab back
here with you-all. I aim to have a clear view ahead
when all I got to see by is a puny moon-ball."

Caldwell frowned. "I thought you didn't know how
to handle that camel of yours."

Greenberg spit again. "I kin do anything, do I have
to. I jest never was a man to do a thing I don't."

MORNING FOUND THE tired men of the camel patrol
skirting the marshy delta of a small braided stream
running from the east into what would have been the
waters of a great salt lake, had the playa still held its
prehistoric contents.

Rabbit-Boss was out in front on foot again, after a
frightened, uncomfortable night clinging to the cantle
of Greenberg's saddle. The braided stream ran to their
left as they moved eastward toward the still-distant
Providence Range. From time to time, Rabbit-Boss
would cut over to the soft ground, stick his wand
in the mud, and gingerly smell. Then he'd grimace,
point his digging stick at the looming mountains, and
start trotting again. Caldwell didn't need Greenberg
to tell him that the water this far out on the playa
was impregnated with mineral salts.

The surface of the playa was gently rolling now.
They were seemingly near its eastern edge, where
long-vanished waves had once ebbed and flowed to
carve the shallows of the nameless, long-evaporated
lake. The Indian spotted something sprouting from the
cracked surface just ahead and knelt to pull what

looked like a blackened twig from the baked clay. It was a dead, salt-poisoned sprig of tarweed. To Rabbit-Boss, this was a good sign. They were coming to the shifting marginal zone where desert life and sterile salts fought their see-saw seasonal battle. They were hours from the playa's edge, but the water flowing to their left would be fit to drink before that. The sun-baked edges of the dried-up lake held little of the bitter salts that settled near the lower center.

Rabbit-Boss jogged on, searching the ground in front of his drumming footfalls part of the time and swinging his eyes up at the mountains on the horizon with every twelfth pace. A row of dark specks shimmered, outlined by the sunrise he was running toward. They had not been there the last time he looked, and Rabbit-Boss stopped, shielding his eyes to peer into the glare. Greenberg spotted the not-too-distant forms at the same time and reined in his camel, calling, "What are they, antelope?" as he unlimbered his saddle gun.

One of the distant figures waved and Caldwell, pulling up beside the scout, gasped, "My God, those are mounted people up ahead!"

Greenberg snapped, "I kin see that fer my ownself, damn it. I make it nine ponies. One of 'em's carryin' double."

"You think they could could be Indians?"

"Don't know. Was you expectin' somebody else out here?"

Caldwell placed one hand on the grip of his dragoon as Corporal Muller rode up to ask, "Orders, sir?"

"Have the men fan out to my right, dismount, and be ready to fire on my command. I think they want to parley. Three of them seem to be coming forward. You'd better move it, Corporal."

Caldwell, Greenberg, and High Jolly remained in position on their mounts as the mysterious riders came closer. Rabbit-Boss stood where he had frozen in place, the deceptive harmless-looking stick resting on his throwing shoulder. Off to the right, the six-man squad were carrying out their noncom's orders in anxious silence.

One of the oncoming ponies broke into a gallop and came in fast ahead of the others. Caldwell raised a hand and shouted, "Steady on! I don't think it's an attack."

He knew he was right as the running pony brought its rider into view, outlined against the sunrise. It was a white girl. Her clothes were in tatters and her cornsilk hair was disheveled and blowing in the wind of her pony's run. She called out, "Don't shoot! We ain't Injuns! The Injuns are lettin' us go!"

Caldwell saw the two behind her were another blond woman and a white boy. Alfrieda Unger's pony shied as it caught a whiff of camel, and Rabbit-Boss ran forward to catch its bridle as the slim girl slid off the Indian saddle pad. She ran over to Caldwell as he dismounted to greet her. She threw herself against his chest and sobbed, "Oh, Lordy, I thought we'd never see the likes of you-all again! Them Injuns kilt Freddy and the Mex and carried us off like the savages they was!"

Caldwell held the frightened child, soothing her with reassuring pats as the other woman was helped from her mount by the young boy and Digger Greenberg. Caldwell's breath caught as he got his first good look at the second, older captive. She was a tall, blond, willowy beauty in her middle thirties, and Caldwell could hardly remember having seen a more stunning vision. Despite her dirty face and trail-soiled clothing, her beauty was breath-taking. Caldwell felt a sick, sinking sensation in his guts as he thought of these two lovely white females in the hands of those filthy Apache. He would never ask, of course, but it was all too clear what their treatment must have been. Jesus, what if either of them was in a family way?

Willy Unger, obviously unharmed and half ignored by the concerned members of the patrol, came over to grab Caldwell by one sleeve and yell, "They still got Jezebel! Ain't you-all gonna git Jezebel away from them rascals?"

Caldwell frowned and squinted into the sunrise as he gently disengaged himself from Alfrieda. The other dots he'd seen were no longer visible. He turned to Ernestine, put a hand to the brim of his hat, and said, "Your servant, ma'am. Am I to understand they still hold another member of your party?"

Ernestine brushed a strand of hair away from her eyes and said weakly, "I don't know. I'm so confused about all that's happened. I thought I'd lost my Willy and then they started yelling at each other and running us all around in the dark . . ."

Caldwell cut in to call out, "Corporal Muller! Break out some water and blankets to spread on the ground for this lady. I do believe she's about to faint."

Willy tugged his sleeve again. "They got my ma's serving wench, Jezebel. The sassy nigger stayed ahint when Eskinya let us go."

"Eskinya? Jezebel?" frowned Caldwell. Alfrieda said, "Hush, Willy, you don't understand. We owe our lives to Jezebel and the way she sweet-talked them Injuns in dago." The young girl dimpled at Matt Caldwell and explained, "We had us a slave girl with us, name of Jezebel. A buck named Eskinya took a shine to her, and when them Injuns got to fightin' amongst themselves, Jezebel got her Injun beau to turn us loose."

"She gave up her own freedom in exchange for your safety?"

"Not exactly. I didn't understand the half of what they jawed about in dago, but the way I understand it, Eskinya told her it was her own free choice to make."

Willy said, "Dang it, Jezebel never had no choice. She was a nigger slave as belonged to ma and pa. If you don't hurry, mister, them pesky Injuns'll ride off with our property!"

Caldwell turned to the oldest member of the family,

a puzzled smile on his face. Ernestine was being helped to a seat on the saddle blanket Muller had spread out in the dust for her. She looked up blankly when the officer touched his hat brim a second time and said, "It's up to you, ma'am. I'm a Free-Stater myself, but I'm sworn to uphold the law as I find it on the books."

Alfrieda sank to her knees at her mother's side and pleaded, "Let her go, Momma! She kept them Injuns from hurtin' us."

As Ernestine hesitated, Digger Greenberg asked the girl, "Did they say where they was headed, missy?"

Willy piped up, "The White Mountains. I understood that much. That sassy Eskinya tolt Jezebel he'd carry her off to the Sierra Blanca, and don't that mean White Mountains in dago?"

Greenberg nodded and observed, "They've splintered off to jine up with Cochise. Last I heard, Cochise was sellin' firewood to the army over by Apache Pass. I'd allow as how this Eskinya jasper hankers fer some peace and quiet, do we'uns let him have it."

Alfrieda shook her mother and insisted, "Momma! Tell these soldiers to let 'em go! Daddy will buy you another nigger if you ask him nice."

Ernestine sighed. "I don't know what to say. It's like I've just awakened from a bad dream. Are we really safe among our own people again? Where are we? Where is my Hansel? I want my Hansel."

Alfrieda Unger looked up at the men around her, and her face was determined for one so young as she said, "You-all just forget about Jezebel and her Injun beau, you hear?"

Caldwell grinned. "Were you on your way to California, miss?"

"To Los Angeles City. What about it?"

"California is a free state. I don't think, all things considered, I should risk a running gunfight with a peacefully inclined Apache just to recover a slave you wouldn't be able to legally hold aginst her will."

Willy Unger scowled. "My pa will surely be pissed off at you, mister!" But Alfrieda leaped to her feet, threw her young arms around the startled officer, and kissed him on the cheek, gushing, "I knowed you was just a darlin' man the moment I laid eyes on you!"

Caldwell flushed beet red as he caught the amused looks of the men around them. He untangled himself a second time from the budding young woman. "After you've had something to eat and drink and a chance to rest up a bit, we'd better see about getting the three of you back to Fort Havasu."

Digger Greenberg spit. "I reckon we'd best start searchin' out a place to make our stand. I see a swell over there where the creek makes that ox-bow turn. We'd best git up on top and lay these camel critters in a circle whilst there's still time."

Caldwell asked, "What are you talking about?" and the scout pointed out across the playa to the west of his chin. Caldwell stared the way Greenberg and Rabbit-Boss were looking and was barely able to make out a shimmering necklace of tiny black beads moving toward them under a cloud of ocher dust. He nodded and said, "I see them. How many of them do you make it, Digger?"

Greenberg said, "About six dozen. 'Course, half of 'em would be women and kids. More'n half's on foot. This desert's took a toll of their ponies. Likely what they was fussin' 'bout, afore they turnt these folks loose."

"Do you think it's possible they've had enough? They may be on their way to join the others with Cochise in the White Mountains. They may have had enough of Diablito and his bloody ways. They may just want to get out of this hellish desert alive the same as us."

Greenberg snorted. "They may be sproutin' wings

and fixin' to jine a Bible class, but I sort of doubt it. Iffen we'uns kin see them, they kin see ussen, and 'though you may not have noticed it, Lieutenant, they's headed right this way!"

A GEOLOGIST, HAD one been there, could have explained how the waters of the long-ago lake, washing for thousands of years against a bank of more resistant clay, had left a low, smooth whaleback rise for the newer creek of mountain runoff to wind itself partway around. The shallow braided stream, though only ankle-deep, would probably discourage a mounted charge from directly north. How Caldwell intended to hold the other three-quarters of his perimeter was less clear. The mound was little more than a giant mud pie, and its gentle sides were not steep enough to slow a determined runner down enough to matter. The ten camels and three ponies were hobbled and forced to lay on their sides, with their possible flailing hooves on the outside of the little living ring of flesh. The patrol members and the Unger family took shelter, if that was the word, in the center. The unarmed Rabbit-Boss was detailed to stay with the rescued civilians and make sure they kept their heads down. Matt Caldwell knew he and his corporal were going to be too busy to worry about them in a little while. Muller was posted on the north side facing the creek. Caldwell braced his saddle gun across Fatima's big dun belly to the south. Digger Greenberg's sharp eyes and buffalo gun faced the oncoming Apache across another camel's side on the west.

The morning sun glinted on silver conchos and the

white stripes Diablito's distant men had painted across their faces. Greenberg bit off a chaw, chewed it soft, and called out, "Listen, ever'body. Them jaspers is used to fightin' Mexicans with muzzle-loaders. They aim to make a feint to spook us into volley fire, then as they see the puffs of our gunsmoke, they'll throw themselves flat to let the balls pass over. They like to spring up after a volley and come in fast whilst they figure we'uns is busy reloadin' with powder horn and ram. So mind you fire ragged and keep them six-guns handy. The onliest thing a six-gun's good fer is the fine surprise it gives an Injun when he thinks you're reloadin' and you blow his fool face off!"

Caldwell raised his voice. "That's good advice, men. Remember to fire on my command and then fire at will. If they charge on horseback, remember to aim at the horse. Any other suggestions, Mr. Greenberg?"

"Sure, let's run fer it. Even doubled up, these critters oughta outrun Injun ponies, and if you'll look again at them jaspers out to our west, half of 'em is afoot and the ponies left is in a sorry state."

"I hope you're right, but you know the U.S. Army never runs away from a fight, Mister Greenberg."

"I know, but you did ask fer suggestions and I reckon you wanted *sensible* ones. That aimin' fer their ponies is a lot of shit, too."

"Mister Greenberg! Remember there are ladies present now!"

"Sorry, but them Injuns ain't about to let you shoot their ponies. They'll leave 'em outten range with the women and kids. Apache mostly fight on foot. You might say as they's Injun dragoons."

"You're the expert on Apache, Mister Greenberg. Do you think we can get Diablito to parley?"

Greenberg frowned and asked, "Parley? What in thunder do we'uns have to parley 'bout?"

"I might be able to get him to listen to reason. We've recovered these hostages, and if Diablito would turn over the actual murderers of those miners and the teamsters of the Unger wagon . . ."

"Great balls of fire! Why not ask Diablito to sign the pledge and give up smokin' whilst you're about it? Didn't I tell you we'd jest chase that ornery redskin till he caught us? Well, we chased him and now we'uns is purely caught! We ain't about to *talk* our way outten this, Lieutenant. You see the way they's spreadin' out as they move closer?"

"I see it, but he may be bluffing. We're a pretty big boo up here on this rise and behind fair cover. He may decide to go around us."

"All right, and what happens does he go around, Lieutenant?"

"We get these people to safety and report Diablito's presence and intentions in this area, of course."

"Well, hell yes, it's of course, an' if *I* kin figure that, I suspicion Diablito kin, too. He'd be a pure fool to go around when he's better off goin' through."

From the other side of the circle, Corporal Muller called out, "I have some skirmishers out to the north, sir. Two braves on foot and out of rifle range across the creek."

Caldwell half rose, spotted the distant figures Muller was talking about, and dropped back down, saying, "Hold your fire over there. They look like a couple of kids."

"Suicide boys," said Digger Greenberg. "Injuns got rules about lettin' kids jine the warrior societies. No Apache kin own a pony or git married afore he's showed the others he's a fool hero four times. Does anybody charge in ahead, singin' his death song and not botherin' to duck, it'll likely be a suicide boy. It's the kids you has to watch fer in any war. It's right hard to kill folks when you're actin' reasonable."

Greenberg noticed another Indian detaching himself from the main body and forging ahead on a limping pony. The others had formed a ragged line a quarter mile out on the open playa. They were deliberately tempting the patrol to waste ammunition, Greenberg knew. He raised his voice to say, "Don't nobody fire at that range. You got mebbe a one-in-ten chance at wingin' a man at a quarter mile, and them Apache cottons to the odds."

He saw the man on the limping pony was nearly close enough to hail, and turning to the rescued captives, he said, "You, Miss Frieda! Crawl up here aside me and see kin you tell me the tale of this jasper on the stove-in pony!"

Alfrieda Unger started to rise, but Rabbit-Boss grabbed her wrist and snapped, "He say *crawl,* my word!"

The girl did as she was told and joined Greenberg in peering over the side of his hobbled camel. The scout said, "Old Rabbit-Boss didn't mean nothin' by the way he snapped, missy, but you got to larn to keep that purty head of your'n down. Now, you see that jasper downslope on that limpin' pony with the white blaze?"

"That's Kayo-Tenay. He's their chief," Alfrieda said.

Greenberg frowned. "Not Diablito? I thought them rascals was Diablito's band!"

"We never heard mention of anyone called Diablito," the girl insisted. "Their chief is Kaya-Tenay. Other big Injuns was called Ki-E-Ta, Eskinya, Naiche, Tso-Ay, Taza, and such. I'm sure if one of 'em had been called Diablito, we'd have heard about it. Our Jezebel got mighty close with them and . . ."

"You hear all this, Lieutenant?" Greenberg cut in. "We got us *two* hostile bands to report!"

Caldwell said, "I know. What do you think that chief on the lame pony wants?"

"Jest showin' off an' killin' time. He's riskin' a useless mount and his own ornery hide to show them others what good medicine he has. He's hopin' we'll jaw a spell whilst he sizes up our numbers and our nerves."

Greenberg braced his buffalo gun across the camel, took careful aim, and muttered, "He's hopin' wrong," as he fired.

Alfrieda screamed as the gun went off near her ear. Out on the flat, Kaya-Tenay flew from his saddle pad as if jerked by a string. He landed on his back in the dust, rolled in a backward somersault, and sprang to his feet as the pony trotted nervously toward the stream. As the Indian ran back toward his own line, Greenberg spit and said, "Only winged the son of a . . . sorry, missy. Anyways, I reckon he's hit in the left lung from the way he spun offen that pony. Danged gun shoots a mite to my right."

Matt Caldwell asked, "Why in thunder did you do that, Greenberg? The man might have had something to say!"

The scout replied, "Shoot, I knowed what he had to say. He'd begin tellin' us he was not a bad man and only wanted to water his ponies in yon creek. Then, after I tolt him no, he'd allow as how we had more brains than to let the whole band git that close without we fired, so he'd beg fer tobacco and gunpowder to keep us jawin' whilst he sized us up and got the others into position and heated up fer a rush. I reckon my knockin' him offen that pony's sort of set their time table back a mite, and anyhow, my Spanish is rusty."

"What do you think their next more might be?"

"That's what they're talkin' over. I see this Kaya-Whatsits has gone back to his squaws and is still on his feet. He's either tougher'n most or I only fetched him a flesh wound. Hope it festers on the mother . . . uh, mean old Injun."

Corporal Muller said, "One of them Injun kids is stompin' around in a circle near the creek, Lieutenant. I think I can nail him at the range he's giving me."

Caldwell said, "Wait until he starts across the creek. I want Miss Unger back with her family if you don't need her anymore, Mr. Goldberg."

The scout nodded. "I'm obliged, missy, but you'd best git your purty head offen the sky line." As the girl started to crawl back to the center of the ring, Greenberg told Muller, "That's a warm-up fer a crazy move, Corporal. Your Injun's singin' his death song and makin' medicine with his Apache gods right now. When and iffen he gits his steam up, he figures to come in fast, touch your camel's foot with the flat of his bow, and run like hell."

Muller frowned and asked, "What would anyone want to do a fool thing like that for?"

"To show the squaws how brave he is, of course. Injuns don't make war like we'uns. It's more like a game to them. You ever play checkers?"

"Sure."

"Well, then you know 'bout givin' a poor player a few free moves to mak the game more interesting. Do an Injun slap at an enemy without hurtin' him, he scores a point and shows ever'body how little he thinks of the hombre he's a fightin'. You see . . ."

But Muller yelled, "Here he comes!" and fired as the painted youth splashed ankle-deep through the shallows of the braided stream. The .44 caliber Minie ball crashed into the Indian's upper teeth, ploughed through between his palate and lower braincase, and severed the spinal cord as it exited via the back of his neck. The lifeless body crumpled in a heap in the running water as Muller yipped, "Hot damn! I got him!"

"Watch his partner," warned Greenberg as Muller started to reload. Trooper Rogers sighed "Jesus!" and fired as the second youth darted toward the fallen boy. He hit the Indian in the leg and dropped him, wounded, a few yards from his comrade. Rogers said, "I'm sorry," and it wasn't clear whether he was sorry he fired without orders, sorry he missed, or sorry for taking the Lord's name in vain. Trooper Streeter said, "I'll get him!" and finished the wounded youth with a round through the chest as Caldwell yelled, "Hold your fire over there!"

Abashed, Muller finished reloading as he murmured, "No excuse, sir. It won't happen again."

Mollified, Caldwell said, "That was good shooting, men. I just want you to remember yourselves, though. We're in a lot of trouble if they all decide to rush in at once and half our guns are empty!"

There was a murmur of agreement around the circle, and Caldwell asked Greenberg, "What does it look like? Do you think they're getting ready for an all-out attack? I don't see how they can hope to take us if they let us whittle them down a few at a time."

Greenberg nodded. "I suspicion they don't neither. Their best bet is to jest lay siege whilst the sun does their work fer 'em."

"Come now, we've plenty of food, and I ordered the canteens refilled before we dug in up here. We can hold this rise indefinitely."

The scout allowed, "Few days mebbe. Nobody knows where we'uns is, so nobody figures to relieve ussen. They got ponies to eat and all the water they need to outlast ussen, and come nightfall, they'll start creepin' in to hit us with plungin' arrows from the dark. They'll be able to make this rise out agin' the stars. We'uns'll jest be lookin' down at lots of black nothin'. I bin sort of hopin' they'd charge us in the daylight, but I suspicion we've taught 'em patience, and yep, they'll wait us out a mite afore they makes another move."

Caldwell stared down at the Indians on the flat, and as if to prove the scout's words, he saw they were building cooking fires and making themselves comfortable. Many of them had spread blanket sun-shades on lance poles driven into the clay, and the women seemed to be feeding some of the ponies from baskets of nondescript fodder. He said, "If we can't get to the creek for water, at least we can keep them back from . . ." and then his voice trailed off as he saw how foolish his first thought on the subject had been. The water soaking into the playa inside the Indians' lines was brackish, true enough, but there was nothing to prevent them from simply going around his position out of range and drawing sweet water from further up the stream to the east. For the first time, he saw clearly just what a fix he'd led his people into.

To the scout, he said, "Maybe we will have to run for it before they have us completely surrounded."

Greenberg shrugged. "Too late. They likely have already. No tellin' how many of 'em there is now ahint them other rises all around. We'uns has the highest ground hereabouts, but it only takes a three-foot swell in the ground to hide most Injuns, and whilst that country out yonder looks dead flat, it ain't."

"Come now. I can see most of the band out there as plain as day."

"I know. It's the Apache you *cain't* see as does you in most times."

Caldwell shrugged and asked, "In other words, we just sit here and wait? You can't think of anything else we might do?"

"If I could, I'da said it. I don't cotton to gittin' run over by Apache any more'n you do."

THE LONG MORNING wore on without further incident, to be followed by an afternoon distinguished only by heat, thirst, and the musty taste of fear in the mouth of everyone trapped on the rise. The sun was in their eyes now as they watched and waited for the Apache to make their next move. But nothing happened. If the Indians had sent anyone upstream for water, they'd done it surreptitiously by circling out of sight of their intended victims atop the mound. The patrol members were beginning to suffer eyestrain in the tricky desert light. The near horizon shimmered, and the center of the playa to their west seemed to be filling up with ghostly water, as if the long-dead lake were coming back to life. As if to add a cutting edge to the thirst they felt on Caldwell's limited water ration, the mirage that afternoon outdid itself in realism. The heat was broken from time to time as another cloud passed over, adding to the surreal quality of the desert light. The drifting clouds cast shadows black as ink in contrast to the dazzle of the sun-baked clay, and it was hard at times to be sure that nothing crept across the desert floor at you but empty shadow.

On the north side of the circle, Corporal Muller watched the two dead Indians in the creek for quite some time before he realized they were moving. He blinked and peered harder at the bodies, half awash in running water. Then he licked his dry lips and said, "Hey, them Injuns we shot are moving! I know they're both dead, but they're sort of creepin' to the west. The current must be doin' it. I think that creek down there is startin' to rise."

"Thunder on the mountains," said Digger Greenberg. The man next to him muttered, "Hey, watch that danged spitting, Mr. Greenberg."

The scout said, "I didn't spit. I ain't been able to spit fer a coon's age," but the injured trooper, Mulvany, insisted, "Sure you did. Right on me hand it was, and I'll not be after tellin' you again. I'm a peaceful man from Mayo, but I'll not be spit on like a gaboon!"

"You're loco," muttered the scout as another man protested, "Damn it! Somebody just spit on *me!*"

Matt Caldwell half turned and said, "All right, let's not have any more of this horseplay. Save your schoolboy pranks for those Indians down there!"

Then something wet plopped against his left wrist. Another great gob of liquid spattered on the barrel of his carbine, and Caldwell gasped, "I'll be God damned —sorry, ladies—but it's *raining!*"

The others laughed in surprise as other drops began

to patter down, and Greenberg said, "It happens out here sometimes. 'Bout once ever' ten or twenty years."

The men looked up at the gray clouds drifting over them from the southwest, and some began to laugh while others took off their hats to catch what coolth this unusual desert weather might provide for the moment.

Down on the flat, the Indians were staring up, openmouthed, at the darkening sky as suddenly a bolt of lightning flashed between the clouds. Another flash, much closer, answered, and without further warning, the rain was coming down in lashing solid sheets.

"Mind you keep your cartridges dry!" shouted Caldwell as the rain came down in a tropical torrent, soaking them all to the skin in less than a minute. The sky was getting darker, and the water in the braided stream was growling like some great prehistoric beast as it began to remember its former station in life as a great river. Someone shouted, "Jesus, it's a regular gully-washin' cloudburst!" and another shouted back, "Thanks for tellin' us. We never woulda figured that out for our ownselves!"

The wind began to pick up as the sheets of rainwater swept to and fro across the playa. The lightning was a nearly constant cannonade, and somewhere a woman was screaming. Matt Caldwell stared out from under his dripping hat brim for a long, long time before he crawled over to Greenberg, nudged the scout for attention, and shouted. "I never heard of a mirage when the sun wasn't shining, have you?"

The scout stared soberly out at the spreading shallow lake to their west and nodded as he opined, "That ain't no mirage. It's real. The goddamn lake is filling up!"

The Indians from their lower vantage point took only a few more minutes to become aware of what was happening. Hurriedly, they began to dismantle their camp, pack their ponies, and start looking for high ground. The nearest high ground, of course, was occupied by the camel patrol. Somebody yelled, "Sweet Jesus, here they come!" as man, woman, and child, Kaya-Tenay's entire band, came up the gentle slope at them!

"Fire at will!" shouted Caldwell as, suiting action to his word, he brought the nearest pony down with a well-placed ball. The trooper next to him finished the rider, and neither commented on the fact that the rider had been a squaw. Cho-Ko-Ley, wife of Kaya-Tenay, had led the desperate charge with a Nadene lance in her upraised hand.

The others kept coming, and shot after desperate shot echoed the louder thunder of the fall rains. The top of the mound was enveloped in a small cloud of its own as gunsmoke made it difficult to see just what was happening. A dim figure dove headfirst over Greenberg's camel and landed dead on Mulvany's boot heels. A screaming man named Naiche loomed above Caldwell as the officer desperately reloaded his spent six-gun with a fresh cylinder. He never knew how close a call he'd had as his camel, Fatima, reacted to the frightening screams by stretching out her long neck and biting the Indian's face off with her big green teeth.

The ragged fire died as bewildered men searched for new targets in the smoke and torrential rain. The wind swept Corporal Muller's field of vision clear for a moment, and the noncom gasped, "Good God!" as he caught a glimpse of the area once occupied by a gentle braided stream. The creek was no longer there. In its place roared a brown and muddy river at least five miles across! As the last of the smoke drifted away, the men of the patrol saw they were no longer on a rise in the desert floor. They were on a slowly shrinking island, surrounded by a vast, rising lake!

Here and there, a frightened pony swam in circles or a human head bobbed above the swirling brown waves. The current was carrying them out to deeper water. There were not that many, for few Nadene knew how to swim. Somebody gasped, "Sweet Jesus! What happened to all them Injuns?" and Digger Greenberg spit again to reply quite calmly, "I tolt you, ever' once in a while it *rains* out here."

IT WOULD TAKE the nameless lake several years to dry up again, but in only a few days the waters around what they'd remember as "Caldwell's Island" had fallen enough for the long-legged camels to ford them to the higher ground to their east.

The trip back to Fort Havasu was easy and without incident. Matt Caldwell had learned to live with Fatima's constant stink and stubborn disposition and, having come to know the Great American Desert first-hand, respected his camel for what she was, the best possible mount for policing the arid lands between the Pecos and the coastal ranges of California.

Captain Calvin Lodge was of a different opinion.

It was the morning after the patrol had returned, with the captives rescued and the renegade Apache eliminated, that the captain called Matt Caldwell to his office for a private conference. He waved his junior officer to a seat, offered him a cigar, and then hooked his rump over one corner of his desk, saying, "I've been going over your report. It seems pretty fantastic, but I suppose you wouldn't want to change any of it."

Caldwell lit up, blew a thoughtful smoke ring, and asked, "What's in there that you don't agree with, Captain? It all happened pretty much as I wrote it down last night."

"Oh, I'm going to write you up for a commendation, Caldwell. The Ungers are safe and sound and on their way to California. You wiped out Diablito and you never lost a man. It was a brilliant action, brilliantly conducted."

"I owe a lot to Greenberg and his Indian, sir, and of course, we couldn't have done it without the camels. High Jolly should be written up for the job he did, too."

Lodge looked uncomfortable. "I'm putting Greenberg and the Digger in for a bonus. High Jolly will be leaving us. He's expressed a desire to become an American citizen and I've expedited it. We're seeing about letting him claim some land along the Gila, and, well, High Jolly will be taken care of."

"I'm sure he'll be pleased, sir. Who'll be taking over in his place?"

"Nobody. The camels are being phased out. The new Secretary of War has decided the fool experiment was a waste of the taxpayers' money."

"Sir, that's just not true! Why, without those camels . . . Did you say *new* Secretary of War, sir?"

"Yes. Jefferson Davis has been fired. Even a wishy-washy half-ass like Buchanan has a little sense, and the rascal was just pushing his Slavocrat conspiracy too damned far. The President finally had to ask for his resignation, and Davis has gone back to Mississippi to rant and rave about his damned states' rights. You, uh, can see where this leaves us on the matter of his camel nonsense, can't you?"

"I'm not sure I can, sir. I'm against most everything Jeff Davis stands for, but to give the devil his due . . ."

"We don't give the devil *shit* when he's an outspoken enemy of the Union, Mister!"

"Well, what do you want me to say, Captain? That I never found the camel patrol concept useful? I mean, damn it, we just wiped out a whole band of Apache with . . ."

"*Horses,* Mister! You rode Diablito down with U.S. Army Issue *horses,* and I want you to remember that when you, uh, go over your report a second time."

Caldwell shook his head. "I can't be party to a lie, sir. I can see why Jeff Davis's enemies in Congress want to make a laughing stock out of him, but . . ."

"All right, let's try it another way. Let's say you simply refer to what you and your men rode on as, well, *mounts*. That would leave your honor clean and satisfy a lot of people in Washington at the same time."

"I guess it would, sir, but if I tell it like it happened, a lot of people are sure going to think we have great horses in our army. I mean, damn it, we drove them nearly a week without food or water and . . ."

"I knew you'd see it my way," the captain cut in, putting a friendly hand on Matt's shoulder as he added, "There'll be citations and promotions for your men, and you do want to help preserve the Union from Davis and those Secessionist madmen of his, don't you?"

"I guess I do, sir."

"Good. I'll tell you what, Lieutenant: suppose I write up the report the way, uh, certain people would like to have it written, and you can just sign it."

"If you think it'll discredit the wild ideas of Jefferson Davis, sir, I suppose I have no other choice."

Captain Lodge slapped him on the back and stood up, saying, "I'll get right on it, Matt."

Matt Caldwell got up, too, and walked over to the window. Outside, Fatima kneeled in the dust, chewing her cud and burbling contentedly in the hot sun. Caldwell wondered what would become of her and the others, and if anyone, ever, would remember the U.S. Camel Corps.

AFTERWORD

In all, the U.S. War Department had purchased nearly a hundred camels in two shipments. When the War between the States broke out, some few dozen were still being kept at remote army posts, neglected and despised as the foolish experiment of the crank former Secretary of War and, to the army, traitor to the Union.

In the irregular guerrilla fighting of the Southwest, some few camels were used as pack animals by both Union and Confederate forces. By the end of hostilities, most had been killed by neglect, butchered for dog food, or simply turned loose to forage for themselves as best they could. Many would seem to have been killed by Indians. Others survived in the rugged dry lands and managed to reproduce themselves for a few generations. Wild camels have been reported as late as the 1940s in the Basin and Range country. Some people still think there are wild camels in the Mojave, and naturalists see no reason why they couldn't be right.

Hadj Ali (High Jolly) lived to a ripe old age as an Arizona rancher. He married an American girl and founded the Jolly family of the Phoenix area. His grave has been designated a Historical Monument.

Raw, fast-action adventure from one of the world's favorite western authors
MAX BRAND
writing as Evan Evans

0-515-08571-5	**MONTANA RIDES**	$2.50
0-515-08527-8	**OUTLAW'S CODE**	$2.50
0-515-08528-6	**THE REVENGE OF BROKEN ARROW**	$2.75
0-515-08529-4	**SAWDUST AND SIXGUNS**	$2.50
0-515-08582-0	**STRANGE COURAGE**	$2.50
0-515-08611-8	**MONTANA RIDES AGAIN**	$2.50
0-515-08692-4	**THE BORDER BANDIT**	$2.50
0-515-08711-4	**SIXGUN LEGACY**	$2.50
0-515-08776-9	**SMUGGLER'S TRAIL**	$2.50
0-515-08759-9	**OUTLAW VALLEY**	$2.50

*Blazing heroic adventures
of the gunfighters of the WILD WEST
by Spur Award-winning author*

LEWIS B. PATTEN

____	**GIANT ON HORSEBACK**	0-441-28816-2/$2.50
____	**THE GUN OF JESSE HAND**	0-441-30797-3/$2.50
____	**THE RUTHLESS RANGE**	0-441-74181-9/$2.50
____	**THE STAR AND THE GUN**	0-441-77955-7/$2.50

![rifle illustration]

The Biggest, Boldest, Fastest-Selling Titles in Western Adventure!

★★★★★★★★★★★★★★★★
CHARTER'S MOST WANTED LIST

Merle Constiner
__81721-1 TOP GUN FROM THE DAKOTAS — $2.50
__24927-2 THE FOURTH GUNMAN — $2.50

Giles A. Lutz
__34286-8 THE HONYOCKER — $2.50
__88852-6 THE WILD QUARRY — $2.50

Will C. Knott
__29758-7 THE GOLDEN MOUNTAIN — $2.25
__71146-4 RED SKIES OVER WYOMING — $2.25

Benjamin Capps
__74920-8 SAM CHANCE — $2.50
__82139-1 THE TRAIL TO OGALLALA — $2.50
__88549-7 THE WHITE MAN'S ROAD — $2.50
